If the Summer lasted Forever

Shari L. Tapscott

ALSO BY SHARI L. TAPSCOTT

Glitter and Sparkle Series

Glitter and Sparkle

Shine and Shimmer

Sugar and Spice

If the Summer Lasted Forever

Just the Essentials

27 Ways to Find a Boyfriend

Fantasy Fiction

Silver & Orchids

Moss Forest Orchid

Greybrow Serpent

Wildwood Larkwing

Lily of the Desert

Fire & Feathers: Novelette Prequel to Moss Forest Orchid

Eldentimber Series

Pippa of Lauramore

Anwen of Primewood

Seirsha of Errinton

Rosie of Triblue

Audette of Brookraven

Elodie of the Sea

Grace of Vernow: An Eldentimber Novelette

Fairy Tale Kingdoms

The Marquise and Her Cat: A Puss in Boots Retelling

The Queen of Gold and Straw: A Rumpelstiltskin Retelling

The Sorceress in Training: A Retelling of The Sorcerer's Apprentice

Writing as Shannon Lynn Cook

Obsidian Queen

Guild of Secrets

Princess of Shadows

Knights of Obsidian

If the Summer Lasted Forever

9781720365570

Copyright © 2018 by Shari L. Tapscott

Editing by Z.A. Sunday
Cover Design by Shari L. Tapscott
Special Thanks to Christine Freeman and Leah Feltner

For everyone who's had, or dreamed of, a summer romance.

CHAPTER ONE

I LIVE smack-dab in the middle of Nowhere, Colorado. Most people know it as Gray Jay, the cutest little summer destination this side of the Continental Divide. Our town is literally named after the gray and black bird that steals everything from picnic lunches to dog kibble. Our economy: tourism. Human population: four-hundred.

We have eight billion trees, no shopping malls, no Starbucks, and only two bars of cell phone service (and that's on a good day).

But what's the worst thing about Gray Jay? The total and complete lack of dating options. I grew up with every guy close to my age, and all the good ones have been claimed since the third grade. The only time there's new blood in our town is May through September, peak tourist season—the months in which Gray Jay makes a living. But you don't want to get involved with those boys —no. They're summer boys, off limits. They'll steal your heart and leave you pining for the rest of the year. Trust me—I know.

But some of us Gray Jay girls still like to browse the summer buffet. Specifically, a someone by the name of Paige, my best friend.

"He's a good kisser," Paige says, leaning against the counter, smacking her gum like a valley girl from the eighties.

Her hair is dark, nearly black thanks to the Cherokee genes on her mom's side, and it's pulled back in a sleek ponytail. I'd kill for her hair.

"Not as good as Bryce but better than Noah," she continues.

"Mmmhmm," I say absently, browsing through our online reservations. My mom owns Campfire Cabins and RV. As the name implies, it's a campground that also rents out cabins. I usually work the front desk during the summer because Uncle Mark runs the property, and Mom's often in her studio, creating small sculptures she sells at one of the local coffee shops.

It's a bright and sunny Tuesday afternoon in late May, one of our slowest days for check-ins, and we only have two spots filling up today. The first is Greg and Hallie Hendrick and their Greyhound, Bark. They'll be staying in Cabin Four, the closest to the creek. Greg likes to fish, so I made sure he could cast a line right from the back porch.

The second is the Tillman family—David, Sarah, and their four children, two dogs, two cats, and a *guinea pig*.

Somehow, they've packed themselves into a thirty-six-foot travel trailer.

When I talked to Sarah a week ago, she said they are "full-timers"—people who live in their RV and travel the country, going wherever they please, whenever they please—and they decided to spend the summer here, in Gray Jay. I have no idea *why* they would want to do that, but I booked them a secluded spot close to the playground, one with a little elbow room. I figured with that many kids and animals, they'll need it.

"Lacey? Are you listening?" Paige asks as I look to see which campers are scheduled to check out, hoping there's not a cabin opening up.

Dang it—Cabin Three. Patty, the woman who handles our housekeeping, has Tuesdays off, which means I have to clean the cabin when the couple leaves so it will be ready for more guests.

"Trev is a good kisser," I say, eyes on the screen. "Better than Noah. Not as good as Bryce."

I have no idea who these boys are, except Trev is a new summer boy, and Noah and Bryce are from past years.

Paige sighs like I've disappointed her somehow. I look up, meeting her dark brown gaze. Feeling guilty, I turn away from the computer, giving her my full attention. "How long is he here?"

"He was a weekend boy."

Weekend boys are even worse than *summer boys.*

She blows a bright pink bubble, and it snaps with a

pop. "But he said his family stays at Upper Ridge several times a summer, so he'll probably be back."

Upper Ridge, also known as the bane of our existence, is another private campground. The sites are crammed together, sardine-style, but they're cheaper. Luckily, we have something they don't—free showers, weekend bonfires with s'mores, and children's activities that I usually get stuck hosting. Honestly, we're both booked all summer, so I don't know why we can't get along.

Paige narrows her eyes, studying me. I squirm, not liking the look. Finally, she says, "You need a summer boy."

"Not again, thank you very much."

"Come on—they're fun. You're just looking at it the wrong way. The *best part* is they leave, and you get to pick another. It's like renting puppies. All the fun, none of the responsibility."

I laugh, incredulous, shaking my head. "You don't even realize how horrible you are."

She levels me with a stare. "Now listen. Almost no one ends up with one of the first guys they date. What if Mr. Forever comes along, and you haven't dated your mandatory three duds before you meet him? Then Mr. Forever will end up with someone else."

"You know what worries me?" I turn back to the computer, remembering I need to print more campground maps. "I think you're serious."

"I *am* serious."

I realize I'm out of paper just before I click the

"print" button. Instead of digging a new pack from the file cabinet, I turn back to Paige. "Mandatory three? Did you make that number up?"

"Yes," she says, not even hesitating.

"I worry about you."

The front door opens, letting in the sounds of birds singing in the trees and a diesel engine idling somewhere in the campground. Paige waves, mouthing a goodbye as she heads out the door, letting me tend to the couple who lingers near the entrance.

"Come on in," I say, smiling as I pull up our check-in screen on the computer. "Are you the Hendricks?"

The forty-something woman pushes her designer sunglasses back, wearing them like a headband in her lush, short brown hair. She has on a loose, lightweight sweater that looks like it cost a fortune, paired with leggings that also look like they cost a fortune. It's an easy, light, I'm-on-vacation kind of outfit—worthless if you're planning on doing anything other than meandering the paved trails and snapping pictures on your phone (which is now a glorified camera because you likely don't have enough service to post said pictures to any of your social media accounts).

I almost sigh, wishing I made enough to buy an outfit like that—wishing I had somewhere to *wear* an outfit like that.

"Actually, we're the Tillmans," the man next to Designer Woman says. He has a five o'clock shadow and the kind of prized genes that must have been passed down from gladiators. Together, they look like they could model for those advertisements you see when you walk into a sporting goods store. You know the ones—where the couple stands in front of a tent, smiling at each other over steaming mugs of coffee—

Hold up. The *Tillmans*? As in four kids and a mobile animal farm?

"*Oh*," I stammer, shocked.

After talking to Sarah Tillman on the phone, I had an image of a rounded, matronly woman in my head. One who wears baggy jean shorts, stark-white sneakers, and massive, floppy sun hats.

"The Tillmans—of course." I smile wider to hide my surprise. "I have the perfect spot all picked out for you. It's a little tricky to back into because of the landscaping, but it's the largest space, and you'll have lots of privacy."

"That's fine," Mr. Tillman says like he navigates his thirty-six-foot camper into tight spaces all the time. Which, since they're full-timers, I suppose he does.

He smiles like he's genuinely pleased to be in the middle of nowhere for the summer and scans the local attraction brochures on the counter.

Mrs. Tillman zeroes in on one of my mother's sculptures—an abstract piece that's called *Wind*. "This is beautiful," she says.

"Thanks." I tap away at my computer, completing the short and simple check-in process. "It's my mom's."

"She has good taste."

"She does," I agree, my smile becoming more genuine, "but that's one of *her* pieces. She's a sculptor."

Mrs. Tillman's eyes widen with surprise. She's just

about to answer when the door opens, and six-foot-two-inches of teenage male perfection leans into the office. "Apparently McKenna fed Candy half a bag of rainbow candies on the drive, and she just threw up in the back seat."

I gape at the sandy-haired boy, my fingers frozen on the keyboard.

"McKenna or Candy?" Mrs. Tillman asks, less concerned than I would be if that statement were directed at me.

"Candy. Now Caleb says he's going to be sick if I don't let him out."

Mrs. Tillman sighs. "Please get Candy out of the car before she has another accident." She turns back to me. "What spot are we in?"

As soon as she says it, the boy turns his gaze on me and finally notices me sitting here staring at him. My mouth goes dry, and no words come out.

Just because I don't want a summer boy doesn't mean I'm immune to them. It's the whole look-but-don't-touch philosophy.

What did Mrs. Tillman just ask me?

Mr. Tillman clears his throat, amused. My cheeks flame as my brain jolts back to life. "Twenty-nine."

Mrs. Tillman turns back to the boy in the door. "Walk Candy to the site. Take Caleb with you—do *not* let him talk you into getting his bike from the rack. We'll take them down when we're settled in."

A smile toys at the boy's lips, his eyes still on me. "Do you have a map of the campground?"

My gaze strays to the empty stand on the counter, and my cheeks get hotter. Unable to look at him, I say, "I just ran out. Let me print you one real quick."

"No worries." A lazy smile finally stretches across his face. "Why don't you show me the way?"

CHAPTER TWO

FACT: I am a competent human being behind the safety of my check-in counter. I can answer the phone, have real conversations, even hand people keys to their cabins. But outside the front office—especially in the presence of a good-looking guy with pale green eyes and an easy way of *existing*—I'm a newborn giraffe.

"Sure." I turn from the counter and promptly trip over my chair.

Smooth, Lacey.

Since my cheeks can't get any hotter, I assume my neck and chest are growing blotchy as well, though I can't check for obvious reasons.

Another fact: my hair is reddish-brown, and my skin is the fair shade that often accompanies that particular color—which basically means I have blushing down to an art.

Turning to Mrs. Tillman, I say, "The showers are open from six to nine. We begin the weekend bonfires at eight, and nightly quiet hours are from ten o'clock to eight in the morning. If you need anything, please let us know."

After that, I scurry toward her son, my eyes focused on the floor as I try not to look as awkward as I feel.

"I'm Landon," he says as he holds the door open for me.

Landon. It's a different name, but it fits his sunshine smile so well.

I tuck a stray lock of hair behind my ear and concentrate on putting one foot in front of the other. "I'm Lacey."

"So, you work here?" he asks.

I glance at him, surprised by the odd question. Apparently, he realizes the answer's pretty obvious because a cringe passes over his face before that easy smile returns.

"My mom owns the place," I tell him, wondering briefly if he's nervous too.

But of course he's not. Why would he be? I mean, *look* at him. He's the epitome of casual hotness. He's the kind that doesn't try...the kind that doesn't have to. Every glorious inch of him is muscle, probably sculpted by countless hours hiking, climbing, and biking, and he's topped it all off with a sun-kissed beach tan.

The Tillman's travel trailer sits before us in the parking lot, taking up an RV spot. A sullen-looking teen boy, about thirteen, stands outside the brand-new Suburban, holding a bejeweled leash like it's going to bite him. A white cotton ball dog strains against the lead, pulling for all her ten-pound worth. And how do I know it's a female cotton ball? Because she's wearing a frothy pink tutu.

"She started hacking again," the boy says, glaring at the dog as he shoves her leash at Landon, "and I didn't think you'd want her to puke on your seat."

"Thanks," Landon says wryly, taking the leash, apparently unbothered to be seen with the canine fashion statement.

Without a word, the boy wanders off, phone in the air, toward our gazebo where we've set up a cell signal booster.

"That's Hunter," Landon tells me, rolling his eyes, and then he motions toward the dog. "And this is Candy."

I would answer, but my attention is on the young boy plastered to the side window. He's holding a hastily scrawled sign that reads, "Please, save me."

"Um," I say, gesturing to the prisoner.

"And my youngest brother, Caleb," Landon supplies. He hands me the leash, which I blindly accept, and then opens the door, shooing the boy back so he doesn't tumble to the asphalt.

The boy sits back in the seat and looks up at Landon. "Can you get my bike down?"

I barely hear him over the sobs in the backseat.

"No." Landon sets the boy on the ground and points at him. "Stay."

Then he turns back to the interior of the SUV. A girl several years older than Caleb, but younger than Hunter, stares at Landon. Crocodile tears run down her cheeks. A massive Saint Bernard sits next to her, taking up most of the bench. From the way Landon pushes him into the back, I don't think the dog is supposed to be there.

"Why are you crying, McKenna?" Landon asks the girl once the dog is out of the way, leaning farther into the vehicle to see her better.

"Candy's going to die," she blubbers, her tears starting anew.

Landon sighs. "Candy's not going to die. She's fine."

"Are you sure?" the girl demands.

"Pretty sure."

Just to remind us she's still alive, Candy starts making gagging noises. I stare at the cotton puff, horrified. Are rainbow candies toxic to dogs?

Several seconds later, the noises cease, and she opens her mouth in a wide yawn.

Finally, *thank goodness,* the elder Tillmans show up.

"Go on," Mrs. Tillman says to Landon, scooting him out of the way so she can comfort her sniffling daughter. "I've got this."

Landon steps back, far less flustered than I would be.

"Where did Hunter go?" Mr. Tillman asks.

"Uh, that way," I offer, pointing to the gazebo. "The cell signal is better over there."

"Ah," Mr. Tillman says knowingly, and then he rounds the Suburban, heading for the driver's seat.

I glance down, looking for the littlest Tillman. He's gone.

Landon notices at the same time and jogs toward the fish pond, grabbing his brother around the middle just as the boy leaps for the boulder at the center of the water—a good five-foot jump. I might be wrong, but I don't think he would have made it considering he's only four-foot himself.

"All accounted for?" Mrs. Tillman calls from her window.

Landon gives his mother a wave, and then the Suburban heads down the winding road, toward the camping area.

Suddenly, it's silent enough to hear the birds again, and I realize I'm still holding the dog's leash. Feeling a bit befuddled, I hand her back to Landon.

"So...to the campsite?" Landon asks, his eyes sparkling with humor when he takes in the look on my face.

Slowly, I nod. We follow the same path the Tillman's took.

"I can practically hear your thoughts," he says after several silent moments.

I look over, taking in his salmon-colored T-shirt and khaki hiking shorts.

"You want to know how we contain all of *that* in one camper," he prods.

Because there's no way to deny it, I laugh a little. "It crossed my mind."

"It was insane for the first few months," he admits, talking to me like we're old friends. His easy manner helps me relax, and I focus on the road in front of us. It's strewn with pine needles, and this section is shaded by the towering trees to the west. Caleb runs ahead of us, jogs back, and then runs ahead again. He's a human version of an energy drink.

"Dad came home from work one day a few years ago," Landon continues, "said he had an amazing idea. Six months later, he quit his job, bought the RV, and we've been traveling ever since. It took some adjusting, but it's been pretty cool."

"So, you homeschool?" I ask, more for the sake of conversation than curiosity. There are more full-time families than people realize. I made friends with a few before I came to terms with the fact that they all leave. It hurts less to keep my distance.

"I finished my senior year a few months ago," he answers, and then he turns his head my way. I can feel his eyes on me, but I continue to look straight ahead.

"What grade are you in?" he finally asks.

"I'll be a senior in the fall."

"Is there a school here?" He looks around as if the building will magically pop up in front of him.

"Our K-12 is about forty minutes away."

"That's a long drive."

I shrug. "My best friend lives five minutes from here. We ride together, so it's not so bad."

"How many kids are in your graduating class?"

Finally, I meet his eyes. "Seven."

His eyebrows shoot up.

"I know." I look away, trying not to smile. "We're a big class. Last year there were only two."

"We lived in a medium-sized city before we decided to travel," Landon says. "What's it like to live here?"

"In the middle of nowhere?"

He flashes me a smile that would make my insides all warm and liquid if I weren't so guarded against summer boys.

"It's fine," I finally answer. "Busy in the summer but quiet the rest of the year."

"No ski crowds?"

I shake my head. "We're not close enough to the slopes to get winter traffic, though we do keep a few of our cabins open during the cold months, just in case."

"What do the local kids do for fun?"

I raise an eyebrow at him. "Fun...?"

He laughs, but before he can press for more, we reach the campsite. Mr. Tillman has already backed in, and he and Mrs. Tillman are trying to decide if they're too close to a tree on the right-hand side before they unhook the Suburban.

Candy begins to bark as soon as she spots her Saint Bernard brother. The massive dog lies under the picnic table, slobbering all over a treat-stuffed chew toy.

"Landon," Mr. Tillman says when he sees us. "Run inside and open the table slide."

I shove my hands into my pockets. "Okay, well. This is you. Obviously."

Landon hesitates, glancing at the RV, and then he gives me a smile. "Thanks, Lacey. I'll see you around?"

"I'm always here," I say, trying to be clever, but then I realize I've informed him I have no life.

His smile grows. "Me too—all summer."

Just for the summer.

CHAPTER THREE

"*ERROR CODE 306. Please remove jammed paper to continue printing,*" a popup says on my computer.

I growl under my breath. First, the printer wouldn't feed the paper, now it's jamming after printing only five pages. I yank at the paper, cursing the junky piece of office equipment in my head.

The front door opens, and Paige comes striding inside, letting in a cold, rainy gust of wind. "I've found my new summer boy," she declares.

She's wearing hot pink flip-flops, her favorite pair of shorts with the diamond rhinestones on the back pockets, and an oversized green sweatshirt she must have swiped from one of her brothers' closets.

"Did you miss that it's trying to snow out there?" I ask, grinning at her. She even painted her toenails despite the sleet.

Paige sweeps a hand over her outfit. "I'm defying the weather. It's almost June. It *should* be warm."

Living in the mountains gives you a different definition of warm. We'd be ecstatic if it got to seventy this time of year. It's in the low forties right now and probably won't get much over fifty.

"Who's your new summer boy?" I ask, abandoning the printer. It and I are not getting along this morning, and we need a little time apart. I can print the maps later. Or better, Uncle Mark can fight with it once he's finished repairing an electrical outlet in Cabin Six.

Paige gives me a Cheshire Cat grin and practically purrs, "Number Twenty-nine."

My shoulders stiffen, and I look down at the desk. "Oh yeah?"

"Have you seen him?" She comes around the counter and swipes a stick of sour apple licorice Uncle Mark keeps stocked just for us.

"Twenty-nine?" I say as if thinking about it. I shuffle several papers without purpose. "That would be one of the Tillman kids."

I feel her eyes on me, but I ignore her and pretend to look busy.

"I dropped my phone when I was running across the parking lot just now," she says. "He saved it for me. Isn't that sweet?"

"Mmmhmm," I say, pretending I don't mind that Landon rescued her in a rainstorm like the hero of a romantic movie. Why couldn't I have met him like that? It sounds a lot more memorable than me walking him to his campsite after his sister's dog got sick in their car.

I catch myself, startled. Obviously, I don't care.

"You *like* him," Paige stage whispers, her voice triumphant.

I jerk my head up, realizing I've been caught in a trap. "What? *No.*"

"You're a terrible liar. So...have you met him yet or only sighed over him from afar?" Somehow, I sense she already knows the answer to that question.

Rolling my eyes, I reshuffle the papers. "We met a few days ago when his family arrived."

"Did you talk to him?" she demands, flopping down into the office chair next to mine and taking a tiny nibble of the green candy. I don't know how she does it, but she can make one stick last an hour.

"I walked him to their campsite." I say it like it's no big deal—like I stroll through the campground with hot guys all the time.

Which, of course, I don't.

"Well, you must have made a good impression because he asked about you."

Again, I jerk my head up—this time so quickly I'm afraid I might have given myself whiplash. "What?"

She grins and does a seated dance of victory.

I'm busted.

"So, we're standing on the porch, right?" she says, wasting no time. "He's soaking wet because he jumped out of his SUV to save my phone, and I give him my most come-hither smile because, *hello*, he's gorgeous. We talk for a few minutes, and when I explain I live not far from here, he asks if I'm the friend *you* were talking about. At that point, I completely lost him." Her eyes sparkle as she points the licorice stick at me. "Lacey, he was sending out subtle questions about you in the freezing rain when he could have been back in his toasty warm car."

A warm sensation starts in my chest and travels to my belly, making me feel off-kilter and a little breathless. I look down at the papers. *Shuffle, shuffle, shuffle.*

"Didn't you say you were on the porch?" I ask, avoiding. "That's not exactly in the rain. Landon was probably just being friendly."

"Oh, it's *Landon,* is it?" Paige laughs. "You're so delusional."

I prefer to think of it as practicing self-preservation.

"Well, no matter," she says, twirling in the chair, holding her candy up like a royal scepter. "From here forth, we shall consider him yours."

And though she says the words flippantly—and though *I don't want* Landon—I relax just a little knowing my pretty, flirty, vivacious best friend won't pursue him.

———

THIRTY-SIX—THAT'S how many flower barrels we have scattered about the property. Thirty-six—that's how many of those flower barrels I'm in charge of planting.

I can't complain, not really. The June day is actually warm, the sky is that ideal shade of robin's egg blue, and I'm not stuck in the office fighting with the printer or cleaning the guest cabins.

My wagon bumps down the paved campground road,

and black flats of petunias and sweet alyssum bounce against a big bag of compost and a beat-up watering can.

I pause in the middle of the road, right by Site Twenty-five, and fix the earbud that fell to my shoulder. Then I open the playlist on my phone and replay Mason Knight's newest single. He sings about the girl who got away, and I sigh with suppressed longing.

I'm not sure anyone will ever feel that way about me.

My eyes stray to the long camper trailer parked in Site Twenty-nine. The Suburban is gone, meaning the Tillman's must be out enjoying the weather. It doesn't matter to me. I didn't take extra time with my makeup and hair because I thought I might run into Landon while planting the flowers. Of course not.

I roll my eyes, silently mocking myself, and tug the wagon to the next barrel. I planted seven yesterday, and I'm hoping to get another ten finished before I meet Paige later. A car slowly rolls by, and I wave at the woman in the passenger seat.

"Looks like you're having fun," she says, leaning out the window. Her hair is short and curled. It's as blond as can be, but judging from her soft, grandmotherly face, I'm pretty sure it went gray years ago.

"Yes, Ma'am," I answer as I fight to remember her name. I checked the retired couple in myself just a few days ago.

Their golden retriever hangs his head out the back window, looking like he's smiling. His name is Todd, and his great, great, *great* grandpa won best of breed at Westminster years ago. (Because that's what's important to remember.)

"Looks like you're doing a good job," she calls as they continue down the road.

"Thank you...*Mrs. Murray!*" I remember just before it's too late. Satisfied, I pull on my bright green gardening gloves and kneel in front of the barrel.

There's a happy squeal from the nearby play area, and the smell of charcoal briquettes floats on the air as a nearby camper prepares lunch. The aroma makes my stomach growl. Mom bought sandwich stuff, but she forgot to get turkey, and I can't stomach the bologna Uncle Mark prefers. But I'm hungry now—I'll have to scrounge for something when I'm finished with the flowers.

I break up the soil, mix in compost and a capful of the organic, granular fertilizer I'm trying this year, and start planting. I'm just about finished with the barrel when the Tillman's door opens. I glance up, surprised because I thought the family was gone.

Landon jogs down the steps and then turns, holding the door open. "Come on," he calls inside. He has a small video recording device, and he points it at the door.

I free a flower from its cell and watch him, trying not to be obvious about it. What's he doing? After several moments, the Saint Bernard appears at the door.

Landon jiggles a leash, but the massive dog yawns, turns around, and then disappears into the camper once more.

"Have it your way," Landon says, tossing the leash aside before he closes the door.

Quickly, I return my eyes to my project, pretending I'm so busy I didn't notice him. He walks around his campsite with that small camera in hand, talking to himself. I plant the last petunia, pat down the soil around its roots, and stand, brushing stray dirt from my jeans.

Without looking Landon's way, I pick up the watering can and walk to the closest unoccupied water spigot. I couldn't find the hose I usually use, so I'm stuck making several trips for each barrel I plant. Luckily, all the sites aren't full. Otherwise, I'd have to go to the spigot by the play area—which would mean walking right past Landon.

I pull the lever, trying to control the flow of water. It's either all or nothing. Since I don't feel like soaking myself, I settle for a meager trickle and let the can fill slowly. As I wait, my mind wanders.

Is Landon still at his site? Was he going somewhere? The Tillmans have been here for over a week—maybe he met someone in town. The thought makes my stomach twist.

I can think of several local girls who'd be happy to keep Landon company for the summer, like Alissa at Mr. Oliver's ice cream shop. She's back from her first year at college and working there for the summer.

A horrible thought flits into my mind: *Maybe he met Gia.*

She's a year younger than I am and ridiculously pretty. Guys seem drawn to her petite, curvy frame. She's barely five-foot, but they don't care. All they see are her big green eyes and...other things.

I push the thought away. Landon has no reason to go to Upper Ridge Campground, which is where Gia and her brother help out every summer for their aunt and uncle.

Water trickles from the top of the watering can, alerting me to the fact that I haven't been paying attention. Quickly, I jump to action.

But my mind isn't on my task. I yip when the lever comes down with a crack and pinches the skin on my palm. Irritated with myself, I hold in a string of unlady-like words. A few escape, but they are pretty mild considering.

Gravel shifts on the path behind me as a certain someone jogs over. "You okay?"

Feeling like an idiot—*again*—I slowly turn, shaking out my aching hand. I smile like I'm surprised to see him. "I'm fine."

My stomach does a little flip when I meet Landon's gaze. A slow smile builds on his face, lighting his unusual, light green eyes. He catches my hand, tugging me to him like we've been friends for years. His smile becomes a frown as he runs a finger over the angry, purple skin. "You got yourself good."

I would answer, but my mouth doesn't remember how to form words.

"You're very busy," he says, letting me have my hand back. He cocks his head to the side, reminding me of Mrs. Murray's golden retriever. His dark blond hair is cut short on the sides and a little longer on the top. He must wear some sort of product in it to keep it out of his eyes, but it looks soft. Touchable.

"Are you aware of that?"

"Hmmm?" I jerk my eyes from his hair. "That I'm busy?"

He's effortlessly stylish, casual yet purposely so. The entire family is ridiculously pretty. I feel self-conscious even though I took that extra twenty minutes getting ready this morning.

"Every time I see you, you're helping customers or running errands or" —he nods to the watering can— "planting flowers."

I shrug. "It takes a lot of work to run this place."

He nods, still studying me. Then he lifts the small camera and nods to it. "Do you mind?"

I eye the lens. "Do I mind what?"

Smiling, he begins recording and focuses on my face. "Tell me about yourself."

I stare at him, incredulous.

His eyes meet mine, and he chuckles. "Just humor me."

"Why?"

"Because I'm stalking you." He grins at his joke and makes an adjustment to the settings. "It's just my thing. It's a nice way to remember the places we've been and the people we meet."

My stomach flutters at the thought of Landon wanting to remember me, but at the same time, my chest constricts because something about the statement resonates with me. Maybe it's not so different being the one always leaving from being the one always left behind.

"What's your name?" he prompts.

I look at his face instead of his camera. "Forgot already?" I tease.

His eyes move from the screen to mine, and they lock. "Lacey."

He's a summer boy, an obnoxious voice of reason whispers in my ear.

"Come on. Tell me about yourself," he prompts again, his tone a hint softer.

"Um. My name is Lacey." I'm breathless from nerves and something more, but I try to hide it. "My grandparents built this campground, and my parents bought it from them about fifteen years ago."

"Do you have any brothers or sisters?"

"No. It's just me."

A wicked grin flickers over his face. "Want a couple? I have extras, and I don't mind sharing."

"That's very generous of you," I say with a laugh, trying to relax.

"Why should people stay at Campfire Cabins and RV?" He changes his tone so he sounds like he's conducting a real interview and raises a single eyebrow, pinning me with a gaze that's full of good humor.

"Because I plant thirty-six barrels of flowers every single summer, and it would be a shame if no one ever came to see them."

He looks at the screen again, watching me without

making eye contact. "And the girl at the front desk is pretty. Don't forget that."

I blink at him, and a startled smile steals across my face before I can stop it.

Landon turns off the camera and looks up, giving me a friendly jerk of his chin as he heads back to his campsite. "Especially when she blushes."

CHAPTER FOUR

MY MOTHER IS an odd sort of artist. If books and television are to be believed, you'd think she'd be scatter-brained and prone to whims. She's not.

Every night, she has a homecooked dinner on the table. (Well, some nights she delegates the chore to me, but either way, it's there, and it's homecooked.) She makes sure we eat perfectly balanced meals with seasonal produce, and there's usually something homemade for dessert, even if it's just a jar full of cookies in the kitchen.

She's big on family time, good grades, brushing your teeth before bed, and grilling her daughter about the "cute" boy that's staying in Site Twenty-nine.

"I'm just saying I saw you two talking," she says with a laugh, raising her hands in surrender. Her hair is red. Not brown with natural red highlights like mine—red. Every day she takes the time to straighten it, smooth it to perfection, and make it shine...and then she yanks it into a ponytail before lunch because it drives her crazy. She's tall and willowy—like an overgrown pixie. I take after her, but at five-nine, she's got two inches on me.

Uncle Mark smiles at his cards, but it's a seasick sort of look, one that makes me think he wishes we would change the subject. My dad passed away when I was six, so Uncle Mark stepped in to help with the RV park so Mom wouldn't have to sell. I have no doubt that he's just as protective of me as my own dad would have been.

He lives in one of the cabins, but he eats with us every night. He dated some when I was younger, and my biggest fear was that he'd get married and leave us. But for some reason, he never did.

"We were just talking." I discard a ten of hearts and tap the rest of my cards on the table, feeling jittery.

I don't want to talk about Landon.

Mark leans forward to pick up the pile, and I shake my head. "You don't want to do that. Mom's about to go out."

Mark looks over. Noticing the solitary card sitting face-down on the table in front of Mom, he pulls back his hand.

"His mom is nice," my mother continues, refusing to drop the subject. "I met her yesterday when I was checking one of the sites. I'm going to let her borrow my sewing machine for the summer."

I fold my hands and set my chin on the table as I wait for her to discard so I can take my turn. "How did that come up?"

Mom shrugs, studying her card, probably wishing it would turn into something that would play. "She asked me about my art, and one thing led to another."

The doorbell rings before we get to my turn. It's almost nine, but we're supposed to have a late arrival tonight. I told the man on the phone to drive right to his site, but maybe he can't find it.

Mark pushes back his seat, but I hop up first. "I'll take care of it."

Instead of a lost camper, I find Paige on the doorstep. "Can you take tomorrow off?"

"I don't think so..."

"Hi, Paige," Uncle Mark says from behind me, setting his hand on my shoulder.

"Hey, Mr. Mark." She grins. I can tell from her tone she's about to go over my head. "I helped Dad clean our garage, and he said Lacey and I can go out on his boat tomorrow. If it's all right with you."

"I have ten check-ins scheduled," I start to protest. "And I have to water the barrels..."

Mom wanders up, smiling when she sees Paige. "I'll water your flowers, Lacey. It's summer—go have fun."

"And I'll take the cart around tomorrow evening to complete the check-ins," Mark adds.

"Then it's a date!" Paige chirps, worrying me. She's plotting something. Before I can drag it out of her, she runs down the porch steps. "See you tomorrow morning."

"Wait, Paige—"

"I'll be here at nine!"

And then she slips around the massive hedge of chokecherry bushes and disappears.

I shake my head as I close the door.

"I was going to ask if she wanted to stay for dessert," Mom says, "but she took off too fast."

"I'll take dessert," Mark unnecessarily says—he's always game for sweets. "What did you make?"

She gives him an indulgent smile and swats his arm. "We're just getting some good strawberries in, so I made shortcake."

Mom's shortcake is the angel food cake variety—homemade, not store-bought. It's amazing. And worth sticking around for, even when she returns to the table and says, "Now, back to Landon."

"I don't think we were talking about Landon anymore," I protest.

"I think you should offer to show him around."

"We're in Gray Jay," I say, pausing to take a bite of strawberries, whipped cream, and cake. "He's been here more than five minutes—he's already seen it all."

She raises an eyebrow and presses her lips together, trying to look stern. She's not very good at it. "I just want you to be friendly to him."

"I have been friendly."

"And maybe the two of you could hang out a bit."

I point my fork at her. "Why is it I get the disturbing impression you're trying to set me up?"

She gives me an innocent shrug that's anything but. "He just seems nice, that's all. And you can't deny that he's easy on the eyes."

"Ew! *Mother*," I groan. It's one thing for me to think it...it's another for her to say it.

Luckily, Uncle Mark seems to agree with me, and he promptly guides the subject to the fact that my mother cheats at cards.

She argues with him, forgetting all about Landon.

But I don't.

————

AS PROMISED, Paige arrives at promptly nine in the morning. She takes one look at me and shakes her head. "No, no, no."

"What?" I look down at my ripped jeans and the T-shirt that was cute a few years ago but is now faded and butter-soft. "Did your dad implement a boating dress code since last year?"

She rolls her eyes, which are lined with just the right amount of eyeliner to make them look exotic. "We're not going with Dad."

I set my hands on my hips, refusing to budge as she attempts to push me back into the house. "He's letting us take out the boat? By ourselves?"

"Sort of." She finally gives me a hard shove, making me lose my balance. "Come on. You can't wear that."

Giving in, I let her drag me to my bedroom. I sit on the bed as she rummages through my closet. I love fashion, I always have, but there's not a lot to dress up for around here. At some point, I guess I gave up.

"This," she says, pulling out a cute, loose gray tank top and a pair of shorts.

"It's not exactly warm yet," I point out.

"So?"

"*Paige.*"

"Humor me," she begs, her eyes bright and hopeful. She only wears the innocent, woodland animal expression on rare occasions.

Suddenly, I have a horrible epiphany.

"You invited Landon, didn't you?" The words come out as a whispered hiss.

Paige's eyebrows jump, and a teasing smile plays at her lips. "I thought you weren't interested in him."

I look down at my bedspread and smooth a wrinkle in the old-fashioned, floral comforter. "I'm not."

It's quiet for three whole seconds, and then she assures me, "I didn't invite Landon."

Oh. Well. That's good.

Twisting my mouth to the side, I study her. It's obvious she's up to something, even if she hasn't involved the boy from Site Twenty-nine. "Then who did you invite?"

She looks down, giving the shirt in her hands a thoughtful look—but she's really just avoiding eye contact. "Jerrett."

"Jerrett?" I say, aghast.

"Gia's not coming," Paige quickly adds.

Slowly, I nod, letting my hackles down. That's the second time the girl has invaded my thoughts in just a few days. Now, don't get me wrong—It's not that I don't like Gia...

Okay. It's that I don't like Gia.

And I know that's wrong—I really do. But she made out with Thomas Wallert last year during a town picnic even though she *knew* he was dating me. You know what her excuse was? She thought I was home with a headache.

Because that makes it all better.

After that, Thomas and I broke things off. Which ended up working out better for me than Gia. You see, not even two weeks later, Thomas's girlfriend from home —the one he forgot to mention he had—showed up and found them together. Better Gia than me, thank you very much.

"Why did you invite Jarrett?" I ask, more curious than anything else. Unlike his sister, Jarrett is nice. He's also been in love with Paige since we were five. Though he was always on the short, scrawny side, he's filled out in the last few years and shot up about six inches. He's cute, but I'm not sure he's flashy enough to catch Paige's attention.

"Their cousin is visiting from Nebraska," she answers, still avoiding my eyes. "I thought it would be fun to welcome him to Gray Jay."

And it clicks. Jarrett didn't attract Paige's attention— his cousin did. And why not? There's nothing Paige likes more than a summer boy.

"So, I'm there to keep Jarrett company while you flirt

with his cousin? Why drag us along at all? You could have just asked him out."

She laughs and takes my shoulders, giving me a lazy shake as she finally looks at me. "It's okay to get out of here every once in a while."

"You sound like my mom." I roll my eyes and snatch the shorts and shirt from her hands. "All right. Let's try this 'fun' you speak of."

CHAPTER FIVE

THE SUN SHINES, warming the graying wooden boards of the floating dock. In contrast, the breeze picks up a chill as it blows over the lake and is downright cold by the time it reaches us. I rub my arms, trying to warm up, wondering how Paige talked me into changing.

She hops into her dad's pontoon boat, impervious to the cold, and stashes a soft-sided, insulated picnic tote under a seat. Her legs are a warm caramel even though it's so early in the year, and they are crazy long. Mine are white and covered in goosebumps.

The boys aren't here yet, and if it weren't for the fact that Paige rode here with me, and I don't want to leave her stranded, I might go back to the campground.

"Don't even think about it," she says, not even bothering to look up from the seat in front of the wheel.

I smile because she knows me too well.

The engine rumbles to life. It's a familiar sound—the

sound of warm days spent lounging on the deck, soaking up the summer sun. Warmer days than today.

"I can't believe your dad's letting us take out his baby by ourselves." I shift my weight between my feet, trying to keep warm by staying in constant motion.

"He knew Jarrett was coming with us."

Jarrett's that type—quiet, responsible. Parents love him, teachers love him...and girls like Paige don't give him the time of day.

The boys show up several minutes later, wearing heavy sweatshirts and jeans. I give Paige a pointed look, and she laughs under her breath, easily reading my mind.

"Tanner, this is Lacey," Paige says, commencing the mandatory introductions.

I give the flaxen-haired boy a wave. He's tall and extremely cute. With his flirtatious eyes and dimpled smile, he looks more like Gia than Jarrett.

"Hey, Lacey," he says, greeting me with an upward jerk of his chin that reminds me of a different boy...a boy that has started consuming more of my thoughts than he should.

Tanner joins Paige in the boat, leaving me on the dock with Jarrett.

"Are you cold?" Jarrett directs the question to me, though his eyes wander to Paige. He frowns as she sets her hand on Tanner's arm. "You can have my sweatshirt if you want."

Poor guy. He seems to understand the arrangement.

"Nah, I'll warm up," I assure him, though it's bound

to get colder when we're cutting across the water, and I might soon regret the decision.

He flashes me a knowing smile, but he's too nice to call me on my ridiculous choice in clothing. "You ready?"

The picture of good manners, Jarrett takes my hand to steady me as I step into the boat. I choose a seat in the back and watch Jarrett as he frees us from the dock. Tanner gives Paige an uncertain look as she coaxes the boat away from the dock.

"She learned to steer years ago," I tell him.

Paige is the youngest of four children, and her brothers made it their personal responsibility to teach her everything they know. Appearances can be misleading. She looks like a cover model, but she can out-fish, out-hunt, out-everything just about any boy but her older brothers. At one point, she was quite the little tomboy. Officer Hilden, her father, didn't know how to raise her any other way.

We skim over the water, talking and laughing as we get to know Tanner. Jarrett's quiet as usual, but I don't mind.

Thankfully, by midday, the day grows warm enough that the cool breeze is welcome. We float around the lake somewhat aimlessly, finally casting the anchor after several hours so we can dig into the lunch Paige packed.

I eat my sandwich, idly watching Paige and Tanner flirt. Not only does Tanner look more like Gia, but he acts like her too. Even though they barely know each other, Tanner's pulled Paige beside him on the bench, and the two lounge next to each other like characters from a Greek painting.

I'm not too worried—Paige can take care of herself. It's Jarrett I feel sorry for. He laughs with the rest of us, but it must be hard watching his cousin move in on the girl he's had a crush on since we were young.

When the sun is low, and the smell of campfires and charcoal briquettes is on the breeze, we head toward the dock. Kids squeal from the tiny state park campground that's tucked in the pine trees by the shore. The spots are small, designed for tents and little popup campers, but they're mostly full. Now that we've passed Memorial Day, Gray Jay is going to be packed with both tourists and people passing through.

I don't mind. This is the time of year I like the most— when our little mountain town comes to life.

Eventually, it comes time to say goodbye to the boys.

"I had a good time," Tanner says as he gives Paige a lingering hug that makes Jarrett clench his jaw and stare out across the water.

She giggles and promises we'll do it again soon.

"Bye, Lacey," Jarrett says, nodding in a friendly way as we part. "Paige."

He walks away, shoulders slightly drooped, brown-haired head tilted down, half-listening to his cousin as they make their way to their truck.

"Isn't he gorgeous?" Paige gushes about Tanner as soon as we're alone. I frown, still thinking about Jarrett, and then turn to her and nod. He is easy on the eyes.

In fact, Tanner is almost as hot as Landon, but

there's one big difference between the two. While Landon's charming, Tanner's a little on the slimy side. He just has a way about him that makes me uneasy. Who knows—maybe it's because he reminds me of Gia.

"Thank you for dragging me along," I say to Paige as soon as we get back to my house.

She slings her arm around my shoulders and pulls me into a tight, one-armed hug. "You're welcome. How about we go again next week?"

"We'll see."

Shaking her head, laughing, she walks across the gravel to her waiting truck. It's a hand-me-down from her brothers, a beat-up, step-side, seventy-two Chevy in faded forest green. From the way they treat that thing, you'd think it was priceless. Paige was elated when it was her turn to drive it.

I watch as she pulls out of the drive, going slowly down the campground road since Mark's a bit touchy about it. I follow her, off to check the flower barrels. Even though Mom said she'd water them, I want to make sure she remembered. It's not her fault if she forgot—she gets busy.

Taking my time, I wander the campground, checking each one. Sometime, we should probably install a drip system.

I finally reach the gazebo, the place where we have a cell booster and WiFi for the guests. Landon's young teen brother, Hunter, sits on a bench, staring at his laptop, muttering to himself.

"Hey." I step into the gazebo just as the nighttime lighting flickers on. "How's it going?"

"Slow upload," Hunter mutters, not bothering to look up. "It's taken all day."

"It's usually pretty decent." I sit next to him, curious to see what he's trying to do. "Well, no wonder. You have a zillion tabs open."

"Four," he corrects.

"What are you uploading?"

"A video."

I make an understanding noise. "How long have you been at it?"

"Five hours."

"Five hours?" I ask, aghast.

He shrugs. Hunter's apparently a kid of many words.

"Why don't you come to the house and finish it up? Our internet is much better."

Finally, Hunter meets my eyes. "You save the crummy internet for the guests?"

From the rotten gleam in his eyes, I believe he might be joking. It's hard to tell with angsty thirteen-year-olds.

Rolling my eyes, I stand, gesturing for him to follow me. "Come on. I made cookies the other day if you'd like to ruin your dinner."

And like every other teen boy in existence, the promise of food is all it takes. He stands, closing the laptop, and follows me back to the house like an obedient puppy.

A delicious smell wafts from the back porch. Uncle

Mark must be grilling steaks, but that's something he usually reserves for company.

"What kind of cookies?" Hunter asks, breaking his sullen silence.

"Chocolate chip oatmeal. They're my—" I stop abruptly when I open the front door and find Hunter's older brother sitting on our couch, browsing through an old photo album. Mrs. Tillman and my mother sit at the dining room table, chatting over glasses of iced tea. They look awfully cozy.

Landon smiles at my surprise. Just how long has he been here?

Mrs. Tillman looks over from the dining room. "Oh, Hunter. I was just about to send your dad to find you. Cassie and Mark have invited us to stay for dinner."

They did?

Immediately, I think of my messy, wind-blown hair and resist the urge to smooth it. Before I can rush into the bathroom to check my bedraggled appearance, a white blur of fluff comes running into the living room, yapping with glee.

Candy leaps up, setting her tiny paws on my legs. If she were a big dog, she'd knock me down. Considering she's no bigger than a stuffed toy, it's sort of cute.

"Uh, hi there...Candy," I say, only remembering her name since she threw up candy the first day we met. That sort of thing leaves an impression.

"She's a Bichon Frise," Landon's sister proudly says, following her dog into the living room. "Down, Candy. Be a good girl."

Surprisingly obedient, the cotton ball drops to the ground.

"A bichon...what now? She kind of looks like a poodle —" I stop when Landon wildly shakes his head behind McKenna...but not soon enough.

The young girl scoops the dog into her arms and gives me a sad look, the kind that says she must educate me. She takes a deep breath and begins, going on about circuses and royalty, double coats, house training, and grooming schedules.

Hunter rolls his eyes and wanders into the dining room, politely asking my mother if he may have the WiFi password. Apparently, he does have manners hidden under that grouchy exterior.

Meanwhile, I gape at McKenna, nodding politely, baffled by the amount of information pouring from the girl's mouth. She's like a canine encyclopedia—she even cites her sources as she goes. Landon stands behind her, his grin growing as she goes on and on and *on*.

Finally, he sets his hand on her head affectionately. "That's probably enough, Kenna Bear."

McKenna deflates, and her shoulders droop.

"That was very interesting," I assure her. "It sounds like you know a lot about dogs. Candy's lucky to have you."

McKenna's big smile returns, and she scratches behind Candy's ear, making the cotton ball's leg twitch.

"Except when you feed her candy and she pukes in the car," Hunter calls to his sister from the table. Never mind about the manners.

Mrs. Tillman hushes him, looking horrified.

McKenna flashes a snotty look at her brother and wanders away, taking Candy out the front door for a short jaunt around the house...and suddenly I'm alone with Landon.

I glance in the dining room. "Where's the big one?"

"George?"

"George?" I repeat, incredulous.

Landon grins. "The Saint Bernard?"

I nod, wondering if he's going to come barreling from the dining room, just like Candy did.

"We left him in the camper," Landon answers. "We coaxed him out a couple times today, and that's about his limit. He's not what you would call a 'nature dog.'"

"Aren't all dogs 'nature dogs?'"

Landon gives me a sage nod. "All dogs except George."

I hear the kitchen door swing open, and Mark calls, "Let's eat."

Landon hollers at McKenna to come back inside, and we amble into the kitchen. I try to pretend all this is natural, that we have campers over all the time, but that's not entirely true. My mom and Mrs. Tillman must have really hit it off.

Along with Mark's steaks and signature grilled corn, there's a huge salad, a plate piled high with Texas toast, and a fabulous-looking lemon pound cake. To pull all this together, they must have planned this early, probably right after I left with Paige.

The food's set up on the counter, buffet style, and I

fall into line after McKenna. Landon's behind me, and I try not to think of how close he is, how normal this seems when it's so not normal.

"Where's your camera?" I ask Landon as I grab a plate and silverware, feigning nonchalance.

"Dead, sadly. I left it at the camper to charge. But I'm not totally lost without it." He slides his hand into his back pocket and pulls out his phone. He moves next to me, putting us both in the frame for a selfie with the food in the background. "Smile."

He takes me so by surprise, he ends up capturing me laughing in the photo.

"Care if I share it?" he asks as he taps another app.

"Um, sure."

He wants to share a picture of us? Together? With his friends?

Trying not to overthink it, I focus on filling my plate. The salad looks amazing. It's not my mom's usual concoction, and it's not her bowl. Mrs. Tillman must have brought it.

Trying not to dwell on Landon's arm as it occasionally bumps mine, I listen to the conversations around us. Mark and Mr. Tillman talk about fishing while Mom and Mrs. Tillman discuss a popular nearby hike. The trailhead is only about fifteen minutes from the campground, and they're making plans for a joint family outing.

But who's going to watch the campground? What's Mom thinking?

Distracted by the adults' conversation, I don't notice when McKenna reaches for a piece of corn with her bare hand. She immediately drops it, quietly yelping. Then she bites her lip, glancing left and then right, perhaps hoping no one noticed.

"They're hot, Kenna Bear," Landon says, teasing but not in an unkind way. He reaches around me and tugs her hand away from her stomach and looks at her fingers. "You okay?"

"Yeah," she says quietly.

Giving her a smile, he plucks a piece of corn from the pile and drops it onto her plate. "Let it cool before you try to pull back the husk, okay?"

She nods and moves down the line.

"Corn?" Landon asks me.

"Sure," I say, feeling unexplainably wobbly after watching Landon's interaction with his younger sister.

He tosses a piece of corn on my plate and one onto his, and then he shakes his hand dramatically, laughing.

I move toward him, pretending to tell him a secret. "Those are hot."

Landon shifts even closer, his eyes bright. "I noticed."

Hunter loudly clears his throat behind us. "Dude, come on. Flirt later. I'm starving."

As they are so prone to do, my cheeks go hot, and our mothers temporarily abandon their conversation to chuckle at us like we're just too adorable. I'm flooded with irrational irritation, and I move along the counter.

Ignoring them, Landon moves near enough our shoulders press together, and he leans close to my ear. "Yeah, stop flirting, Lacey. Hunter's hungry."

I turn his way, mild retort ready on my tongue, but

then I meet his eyes and realize my mistake. He's so close. In fact, if we weren't in a room full of his family and mine, I might think he was going to kiss me.

My stomach flutters at the thought, and I look away, forgetting what I was about to say. Luckily, Landon's youngest brother bounds up with a book clenched in his small hands.

"Guess what?" he says to Landon in a normal voice before he dons a deep, pirate-esque accent. "There be gold in them thar hills."

"Oh yeah?" Landon plucks the book from his brother's hands and reads, "*Colorado Treasure: Legend of Gideon Bonavit.*"

Caleb looks up at him, his eyes wide with unbridled, youthful excitement.

"It's a local legend," I explain. "He was a settler in the mid-eighteen hundreds, had a claim not far from here. He came to town one day, boasting that he found a huge vein of gold. He was elated because it meant he could finally send for his family. After he left town that afternoon, no one heard from him again for weeks. When someone finally went looking for him, they found him and his wagon at the bottom of a cliff. They think he went over on his way back home."

"That's a lovely tale," Landon deadpans.

I bark out a laugh, agreeing. It is sort of awful.

"Did he have his gold with him?" Caleb asks.

"No one ever found the gold he claimed he'd discovered, and lots of people have searched."

"I want to look for gold!" Caleb snatches the book back and holds it to his chest.

"Gideon's family donated the parcel of land to the Forest Service in the fifties," I tell Landon. "You can take him up there to look around. There's a shanty and signs with info. It's kind of like an open-air museum."

"Sounds like a date," Landon says. "When do you want to check it out?"

I open my mouth, about to protest that I didn't mean *we* should go, when Mom says a little too eagerly, "Oh, that sounds fun, Lacey. Why don't you go tomorrow? It's supposed to rain again this weekend."

"I took today off," I remind her.

She shrugs. "It's summer."

That's right, *summer*. The busy season.

"I need to—"

"We've got it, hon," Uncle Mark says, cutting me off. "Don't worry about it."

Landon gives me a crooked grin. "Well, then. Tomorrow it is."

CHAPTER SIX

I PEEK OUT THE WINDOW, watching for Landon, past nervous. But it's fine. This is just a *casual* outing between *casual* acquaintances. Plus, it's not a date if an eight-year-old boy comes along.

Unlike yesterday, I'm dressed for the weather, wearing layers I can shed as the day warms. I did, however, curl my hair before I pulled it up into a ponytail. And I put on some subtle makeup. If I pulled it off, my skin should look dewy, my eyelashes miles long, and my lips kissably soft. (It takes longer to put on makeup that makes you look like you're *not wearing makeup* than getting ready for an evening date—not that I've gone on many dates, in the evening or any other time.)

The doorbell rings, and I jump a foot into the air like a high-strung cat. Scolding myself, I open the door, hoping it's not obvious I was just pacing the living room.

"Morning," Landon says, looking more inviting than any boy should. With his defined shoulders and muscular build, it's obvious he works hard to stay fit, even on the road. His arms are casually crossed over his almost-fitted T-shirt, and his biceps fill out the short sleeves in a way that would have some girls drooling.

Not me, of course. *Some* girls. Other girls.

"Bring your camera?" I ask.

He reaches into his back pocket, producing the small video recording device he was using the other day. "All charged up and ready to go."

"Your dad says there's a ghost town nearby." Caleb shoves his way in front of Landon. He looks like a miniature explorer in his oversized khaki hat with its wide brim. "Can we see it too?"

"Sure," I say, though my heart twinges when Caleb assumes Mark is my dad and not my uncle.

I walk them around the back of the house to the spot where I park my Jeep. It's a white Wrangler, cute as can be even though it's almost ten years old. When I got my license, Mom and Uncle Mark bought it for me from the lady who owns the rock and mineral shop on Main.

I glance at Caleb, wondering if he's visited the little shop yet. She has all kinds of minerals, even a few fossils. I could buy him a geode, and Landon could split it. And maybe when it's warmer, we could—

I stop myself, realizing I'm planning *more* outings. This is dangerous. The last thing I need to do is get attached—to either of them.

"Nice Jeep," Landon says, earning copious amounts of brownie points.

I flash him a smile. "Thanks."

Five minutes later, we're navigating the winding road, making our way up the mountain. The new foliage on the trees and bushes is rich green thanks to all the rain we've had. Even the pines look more vibrant. It's a pretty day. There are only a few wispy clouds in the sky, and it's already warmer than yesterday.

A creek runs next to us, and Caleb presses his nose to the window. "Can we pan for gold?"

"Some people do, but there are rules and regulations. Your mom and dad would have to contact the Forest Service first and figure all that out."

"Huh," Caleb answers, less interested.

It takes another twenty minutes to reach the turnoff for the historic site—which translates to twenty minutes of mindlessly answering Caleb's questions as I try not to focus on Landon sitting in the seat next to me. His long legs are stretched out in faded jeans that fit just right, and he wears sunglasses and a well-worn baseball cap. He's the embodiment of a Colorado summer.

Finally, I take a right off the scenic highway, turning onto a well-traveled dirt road. It's narrow with bumpy washboards that make Caleb say, "ahhhhh," just so he can hear his voice vibrate.

"It's rough," Landon comments, turning my way as the Jeep's back-end shimmies on a turn. Once we're out of the corner, I glance at him, wondering how he's handling the drive. To his credit, he doesn't look too concerned.

"Soon a road grader will come through," I tell him, "clean it up for the summer tourists in their low-clearance cars and two-wheel-drive vehicles. Paige's brothers *hate* the road grader."

"Paige is your friend, right? The one I met the other day?"

"Yeah." I flash him a smile. "She's the best. I'm lucky to have her."

"I would say she's probably pretty lucky to have you too."

He has no idea. Paige lost her mom just a year before I lost my dad. We understood each other in a way no one else could, and we've been inseparable ever since.

We reach the historic site a minute later, and I pull to the side to park. Caleb scurries out of the Jeep as soon as I turn off the engine, and he books it to the shanty that stands twenty yards from the road.

"Don't touch anything!" Landon hollers out his window, and then he turns back to me with a small smile on his face. He relaxes in his seat, and after a moment, he says, "Hi."

The way he's looking at me makes nervous butterflies stir in my stomach. "Aren't we past that part of the outing?"

"We've had an eight-year-old chaperone."

Which makes me wonder how he would have greeted me if Caleb hadn't been with us.

"Well, then...hi," I end up saying, feeling off...but in a rather pleasant way.

"Thanks for driving us up here."

"Sure." There's a sudden lack of air in the Jeep, so I open my door and step out just so I can catch my breath.

I jam my hands in my pockets as we trail after Caleb. He bounces from sign to sign, reading each one out loud, utterly fascinated.

A Steller's jay, a cousin to our town's namesake, cackles from a nearby stand of pine trees. The greedy thing is probably hoping we'll leave food.

"This must have been a crazy place to grow up," Landon says as Caleb gazes at the small mine Gideon Bonavit dug himself. It's blocked off, but the Forest Service has constructed thick plastic at the entrance so you can see inside if the sun is just right.

"It was pretty cool." My words are contradicted by my listless shrug. Landon gives me a knowing look, and I laugh. "I mean, I like it here—it's home, after all—but someday I'd like to look out my window and see something other than pine trees."

"Have you thought about college? Technically you could leave in a year, go anywhere you want."

"I don't know." I always feel uncomfortable when the subject comes up. "Mom needs me to help run the campground. I can't just leave."

Landon studies me, neither judging nor questioning. It's more like he's trying to figure out who I am. I'm not used to people looking that closely, and the attention makes me fidget.

"I'll probably do online classes or something," I say when I can take it no longer. "What about you? Do you start college in the fall?"

Landon furrows his brow. "I think I'm going to take a year off, travel a little more. But after that, yeah."

"Sounds nice," I say, my tone a touch wistful. The idea of traveling, visiting all the places other people in the campground seem to go to on a regular basis, would be awesome.

We stop by the shanty and Landon peers in the windows, looking at the scene that's been reconstructed inside. There's a tiny cot, a pickax, and a small table with a tin cup and kettle on it—not a lot considering Gideon lived here two years.

"If you could go anywhere," Landon asks me after he reads the sign. "Where would you go?"

"The beach," I say without even thinking about it. "I want to see the ocean more than anything."

Startled, he looks at me, his eyebrows raised. "You've never been to the ocean?"

I shake my head.

"Where have you traveled?"

"Nowhere, really," I say with a laugh. "I have an aunt who lives in New Mexico. We visited her once when I was little, just after my parents bought the campground from my grandparents. I don't remember much about the trip, but apparently, I was terrified of the bats at Carlsbad Caverns."

In fact, the thought of caves still makes me edgy.

Landon looks up from the sign and meets my eyes. "I want to hide you in the RV and take you everywhere."

He says the words lightly, but my stomach warms.

"Maybe to a beach?" I ask, playing along.

"Lots of beaches." His voice is lower, and like magnets drawn to each other, we shift closer. His eyes are

53

the most mesmerizing shade. I don't think I've ever seen a pale green color quite like them.

"Landon!" Caleb shouts. "Look at this!"

Landon clenches his eyes shut, chuckling under his breath. "Be right there," he calls.

Both disappointed and relieved, I step away, putting space between us.

We spend another thirty minutes looking around, taking the short hike to a scenic point that looks out over dozens of natural lakes hidden in the trees. Caleb reads all the signs to us even though he's already been to each one twice.

I stay out of the way when Landon takes out his video recorder. He narrates like he's going to send the video to friends or family back home. He explains where he is, what we're doing, who he's with.

"Wave, Lacey," he commands, pointing the lens at me.

I give in, pursing my lips to hold in a nervous giggle, and do as he requests.

After a while, we take Caleb to the ghost town that's just a little farther up the main road and let him explore the aged, wooden houses.

"I haven't been here in years," I say to Landon as we walk through a two-story that's in better shape than most.

"They're tiny." Landon motions to the room around us. "Can you imagine living somewhere this small?"

He's right. The structures were built in the eighteen-hundreds, and they look more like large playhouses than real homes. There are a few plaques on the walls that talk about who owned the houses, how long they lived there, and what they did for a living. Most of the men worked at the crumbling lumber mill down the road, but a few were miners, and others raised livestock.

"Don't go upstairs," Landon calls to Caleb, who's already climbed the first two steps. "It doesn't look stable."

The boy looks back at his brother, frowning like he's trying to decide if taking a peek would be worth getting in trouble. After a moment, he gives in and comes down to join us.

We wander for a while longer. Growing worried about the way my nerves hum when Landon comes close, I keep a reasonable distance, never letting myself stand near enough to accidentally bump his arm or let our fingers brush.

Over and over, I remind myself this is just a friendly outing, nothing more. The Tillmans are going to leave at the end of the summer. Landon will move on, and I doubt he'll even remember me by this time next year.

This is just a nice way to pass a day—no reason to overthink it or put more stock into it than it deserves.

I'm quiet on the way back, but if Landon notices, he doesn't mention it. Caleb's gregarious enough to carry on a conversation for all of us, and I'm relieved he's here to fill the silence.

We pass Uncle Mark and Mr. Tillman as we pull into the drive. They're standing by the front gate, talking. They wave as I drive around the house.

Caleb hops out of the Jeep as soon as I stop, eager to

tell his dad about the shanty and the ghost town, leaving Landon and me alone—and acutely aware of it.

"That was fun," Landon says.

I play with my keys, purposely avoiding his eyes. "It was. I think Caleb had a good day."

Landon murmurs an agreement. It's hard to get a read on him. He's usually charming, but now that it's just the two of us, he seems hesitant.

"I think we're supposed to go on that hike soon," he says after a long pause. "Mom said she and your mom settled on a day."

"Oh, that's right." I nod.

Silence.

We sit here for another moment, but when it's obvious we've both lost our words, I force an easy smile and step out the door. Landon does the same, though he looks reluctant to join his brother. After a moment, he taps the Jeep's roof twice. "Thanks again."

"No problem." I'm relieved he's finally leaving...and disappointed he's finally leaving.

He pauses on his way toward the front of the house and turns back. "So, I'll see you tomorrow?"

I think about it for a moment, wondering if we planned something I didn't realize. "Why?"

Landon walks backward and flashes me a crooked grin. "Why not?"

CHAPTER SEVEN

"YOU'RE SERIOUSLY NOT GOING to come?" I demand into the phone.

When Mom was planning the family hiking trip with Mrs. Tillman the other night, I figured she'd eventually come to her senses and remember she has an entire campground to run. But no.

She says Jack, a guy from the Silverton area who helps Mark out on occasion, is looking for some extra work now that he and his wife, Kinsley, are expecting their first baby. Jack said he'd be happy to keep an eye on things this afternoon while he makes repairs to the irrigation shed.

I still think it's a bad idea. What if we have a problem with the code to the pool gate like we did last year? Or what if someone runs into the office with the back of their trailer like the year before that? One of us should be here, just in case.

Granted, it's still a little too chilly to swim, so no one's using the pool yet. And the chance of someone hitting the office twice is rather slim-to-none. But still.

"I'm sorry, Lacey," Paige says, sounding sincere. "Tanner called fifteen minutes ago, and we made plans."

"But I need you," I whine.

Mom's been pretty pushy about me spending time with Landon, and I now I know why. Last night, she said I've become a curmudgeon since Thomas, and she wants me to "move on, leave my hobbit hole of an office, and get some sun." (Those were her exact words.)

But Landon scares me. He's too appealing, too quick to smile—too different from Thomas, and I'm drawn to it. But that doesn't mean I can trust him, so it's best to keep my guard up and avoid him altogether. And what if he really is a nice *single* guy? He's still going to leave at the end of the season, just like everyone leaves.

There's something else, too. The other day, when we got back from Gideon's shanty and the ghost town, Landon's mind was somewhere else. He didn't make a move when Caleb leaped out of the Jeep, and he certainly could have if he wanted to. He doesn't need my mother's assistance—chances are he just doesn't like me that way.

And the thought of her interfering makes me want to hide in a hole.

"Landon and I need a buffer, someone to change the subject anytime my mother becomes too pushy," I tell Paige.

She laughs. "He has three younger siblings. How much more of a buffer could you require?"

The girl has a solid point.

"You'll be fine," she assures me. "It's just a picnic and a hike. One little afternoon."

She's right. I can do this.

———

"DO YOU HAVE A DOG?" McKenna asks as we walk down the trail. She's decided she's my best friend, and that suits me just fine. The less contact I have with Landon, the better. Though Mom's been thankfully casual about it, I know she's watching us this afternoon, waiting for a sign that we might like each other.

She's usually so calm and down-to-earth, but I swear she's turning into one of those pushy mothers from a Jane Austen book. I won't be surprised if she starts warning me about the trials and tribulations of spinsterhood before I even turn eighteen.

"No," I answer Landon's sister. "We had a retriever mix when I was younger, but she passed away several years ago."

Her name was Sunny, and she was my dad's. It was a hard loss.

"How come you didn't get another one?"

I glance at the girl—or more specifically, at the white dog lounging in her arms. "Dogs are a lot of work, especially puppies."

59

"You could get a Saint Bernard like George. He doesn't do much."

Ahead of us, just to prove McKenna's point, George decides to lie down in the shade. He paws at the ground, fluffing up a section of dirt, and flops down with a grunt. Dirt collects in his jowls, making a muddy, slobbery mess.

I eye him, internally cringing, but say, "Maybe."

Maybe not.

There's a waterfall up ahead, and Caleb's already taken off, running as fast as his eight-year-old legs will carry him.

"Careful!" Mrs. Tillman yells, but Mr. Tillman only laughs.

Obeying his mother, sort of, Caleb slows to a jog. Candy struggles in McKenna's arms, desperate to run with him. McKenna sets the dog down but holds her back, happy to mosey her way down the trail.

Today, Landon's sister has on hot pink hiking sneakers and a sparkly white vest that matches Candy's rhinestone collar. Something tells me trail jogging is not Landon's sister's idea of a good time. She's happy to go her own pace.

A few minutes after everyone else, we reach the waterfall. It's warmer today, but the mist is a touch cold. Still, Caleb looks like he's about to wade into the crystal-clear pool of water.

Mr. Tillman playfully tugs on the hood of Caleb's sweatshirt and says, "Don't even think about it."

Irritation flashes over Caleb's face, but it's gone as

quickly as it comes. He turns to Uncle Mark. "Do you think there's gold nearby?"

Mark shrugs. "It's hard to say what's hidden in the rock."

The boy eyes the ledge behind the waterfall, looking very much like he wishes he'd brought a pickax. Heaven help us all if he ever finds a way to get his hands on one.

McKenna takes Candy to the water's edge. Prim and proper as can be, Candy sniffs the water and delicately bats it with her paw. Looking positively scandalized, she backs away.

"You're sure that's a dog?" I say quietly to Landon when he steps up next to me. "Maybe she's actually a cat under all that fluff."

"Might be," Landon jokes. I think he knows I've been keeping my distance, though I doubt he's realized why.

"Lacey and Paige used to leap from rock to rock to get over there," Mom tells Landon's mother, motioning to the almost perfectly spaced stones in the middle of the water that lead to a ledge that goes behind the waterfall.

"Used to?" Landon asks.

"I fell in once," I explain, "and realized just how cold that water is."

"Go on, Landon," Mr. Tillman coaxes. "Your camera is waterproof. Film a little."

Landon crosses his arms and gives me a sideways sort of look. "How cold are we talking?"

"In June? With the last of the snowmelt coming down?" I don't bother to hide my grin. "Pretty cold."

"Go with him, Lacey," Mom says. "Be brave."

I shoot her a look, but her eyes are bright. She knows I'm onto her.

"Yeah, Lacey," Landon says, mimicking but not in a rude way. "Be brave."

I know I shouldn't—it would be playing right into Mom's hand, but I haven't been back there in ages, and it is awesome to see the backside of the falls.

"I want to go too!" Caleb exclaims.

"That water's moving a little too fast for you, buddy," Mr. Tillman says. "Maybe in a few years."

And like a fool, my heart gives an extra, hopeful thump. Does that mean the family plans on returning to Gray Jay? Maybe they'll come back every summer like so many of the retirees do.

But that doesn't mean Landon will be with them. Soon, he'll be on his own, in college, and his family will have to travel without him.

"What about you, Hunter?" Landon asks.

His younger brother looks at the falls with disinterest and then shakes his head like the whole outing is lame. Oh, he's at an obnoxious age.

"I'll go," I say, finally giving in.

I feel Mom beaming, but I ignore her and leap to the first slick rock. Once I'm steady, I look back at Landon. "Wait until I'm on the next one before you start."

"Why?" He grins. "Are you worried I'm going to invade your rock and knock you into the water?"

I give him a grim smile, not acknowledging his teasing with a response, and jump to the next rock. My arms circle as I try to catch my balance. It was easier when I was little—when I didn't know how cold that water was and therefore wasn't quite so hesitant to fall in.

Landon jumps to the rock behind me with ease, and we make our way, playing an awkward game of follow the leader. It takes us several minutes, but we finally make it to the ledge. Everyone cheers for us as Landon makes the last leap. He bows his head, accepting their laughing congratulations.

It strikes me again just how good-looking he is.

I bite the inside of my cheek, trying to ignore the funny tightness in my chest, and step behind the water-fall. It's cool back here, to the point of being cold, and the rocks are always wet. Moss grows in patches, and the smell of mineral-rich soil is heavy in the air.

There's a cutout in the rock, not a cave but a recess, and the sound of the crashing water is amplified. Sunlight shines through the wall of water, creating rainbows on the rising mist.

"This is pretty incredible," Landon says, raising his voice so I can hear him.

I look around, feeling nostalgic.

"My dad brought me here for the first time when I was only five," I find myself telling Landon, though I'm not sure why. Maybe because he's the only one here. "It was autumn, when the falls were lazy, and he carried me across the boulders on his shoulders."

I close my eyes and breathe in deep, letting the smells and sounds trigger the memory of him in a way that nothing has in a very long time.

When I open my eyes, I find Landon watching me

with an enigmatic look on his face. Feeling a little emotional, I laugh to stave off the tears. It's been so long since Dad passed. I'm not sure why it's hitting me so hard now.

"Your hair is awesome," Landon finally says, cocking his head to the side, studying me in the misty, filtered sunlight.

I can feel myself blushing, and I raise a hand to my ponytail. "It does strange things in humidity."

"The color is really pretty." He steps closer. "In certain lights, it's almost red."

"It does that." Unsure how to answer, I sort of shrug. I hope it doesn't look as awkward as it feels. After a moment, I gesture to the falls. "Weren't you going to film a little?"

As if remembering, he steps back and digs his hand into the cargo flap of his hiking pants. "Right."

I watch as he scans the waterfall, moving slowly, and then he turns the camera on me.

Rolling my eyes, grinning because it's so hard to have the lens focused on me, I give him a wave. He smiles, pleased, and moves on.

It's too loud to narrate, so he stays silent as he pans the scene. After a minute or so, he turns the camera off. Once again, it's just us. Even though our families are on the other side of the falls, it feels private back here, like we're in our own fairytale world.

It's actually sort of romantic, the perfect setting for an unforgettable first kiss.

Because my mind wanders there, and because I don't trust myself, I step away. "We should probably go back."

"Yeah," Landon agrees.

I sigh with relief as we step out from behind the watery curtain and into view of the others. At the same time, a part of me is disappointed we didn't stay just a bit longer.

CHAPTER EIGHT

"HERE'S your map and the code to the bathrooms and showers," I say to the couple at my counter. "Enjoy your stay."

Mom comes into the front office as they're leaving, and she holds the door open, welcoming them to the park.

"I'm working in the coffee shop for Betta while she drives her dad to the doctor," Mom says when we're alone. Her hair is up in a cute French twist, and she even has dangling earrings in. "I have to leave now, but I promised Sarah I'd get her this book today. It took me a while to find it. Will you take it to her?"

She sets a sewing guide on the counter, one that promises you can make a quilt in twenty-four hours. That seems ambitious.

I rub my ear, turning back to my screen. "Right now?"

"Would you stop avoiding that boy?" Mom says in a tone that's half a laugh and half a scold. "He's sweet, and he must be bored to death. You of all people know Gray Jay isn't the most thrilling place for a teenager to spend their summer."

I give her a look.

She slaps the counter. "*Take the book*, Lacey."

Resisting the urge to pull a Hunter and sulk, I do as I'm told. "Yes, Ma'am."

"Good girl," she says like I'm either three years old or a dog. With a breezy "love you," she's out the door.

In the last week, I've done a spectacular job of avoiding Landon. It's not that I don't like him—I do. He's funny and sweet, and heaven knows he's cute. But that's the problem.

Every time I see him, my breath catches, and my stomach flutters. I know it's just a crush, something meaningless, but I don't want to feel that way about him or anyone else.

Though I continually tell Paige I don't want a summer boy, in truth, I'm not sure I want a boy at all. Better to guard your heart, end up alone, than have it broken over and over. Whether they leave you specifically or just leave Gray Jay, the result is the same. It still hurts.

Hoping the Tillmans are gone, I walk the campground road, taking my time, checking my flowers on the way to Site Twenty-nine. The Suburban's gone, which gives me hope, but if I've learned anything, it's that Landon doesn't always go with the rest of the family on their outings.

The Tillmans have a simple set up compared to some

of the other campers. They have no outdoor lights, no signs, and—thank goodness—no plastic flamingos. They have a woven rug in front of the door, a cheerful one in red and white. A few bikes lean against the picnic table, but the others are on the rack on the back of the trailer, out of the way. A small tent stands near the rear of the site, and it's crammed full of Caleb and McKenna's toys. Their site practically screams happy family.

I come to a stop in front of the door, debating whether I should knock. I don't want to upset George and Candy if they're in there.

As I'm standing here, with the book held tightly in my arms, Landon comes walking down the campground road, talking into that video recorder again. He has it on a selfie stick today, and I desperately want to tease him about it...but that might be considered flirting, and I just can't go there.

"Hey." A smile lights Landon's face when he sees me. "What are you doing here?"

I hold the book out in front of me. "My mom wanted me to drop this by, but I wasn't sure if you were here. I didn't want to disturb the dogs."

Landon retracts the stick, turns off the recorder, and heads my way. He must have had his hair cut in the last few days. It looks a little trimmer on the sides and shorter on top, though there's still plenty of it to run your fingers through.

I blink *that* distracting thought away.

"You've been avoiding me," he says, smile firmly

affixed on his face. He walks my way, advancing on me like a panther.

Shaking my head, I take a step back. "No..."

"Why?" He's close now, just a couple feet away.

"Why what?" My eyes fall to his chest. His T-shirt is faded navy with a weathered twenty-four on it. As far as I know, it's just a meaningless, random number, but my eyes zero in on it.

"Why are you avoiding me, Lacey?"

I rip my gaze from his shirt, making myself meet his eyes. "I don't have..." I trail off, not wanting to make a fool of myself by saying, *I don't have flings with summer boys*, because that would be me assuming he's interested in me. And I don't know—maybe he's just indulging in some casual flirting to pass the time. Maybe it doesn't mean anything at all.

Maybe I'm reading too much into it.

He raises a sandy brow. "Friends?"

I bark out a laugh. "Yes, Landon, I don't have friends. That's exactly what I was going to say."

"Well, if you weren't going to say that, you were going to say something else." He gives me a sly grin. "Which means you're okay with us being friends."

"Are we six now?" I tease, and then I make my voice a higher pitch. "Will you be my friend, Landon?"

"Why *yes*, Lacey, I will be your friend." His voice deepens, taking on an almost sultry tone. I realize I foolishly stumbled into a game without learning the rules first.

I set my hands on my hips, biting back a smile.

"I guess that means you're going to stop avoiding me, right?" he asks. "And we should go to lunch because that's what *friends* do when *friends* are starving. And Lacey" —he leans down, meeting me at eye level— "I'm starving."

I can't help it; I laugh, finally giving in—not to the crush, but to the boy. It's not like I'm going to fall head over heels for him just because he's hot. That's ridiculous. I'm made of stronger stuff than that...at least I'd like to think I am.

"We have one tiny problem," I say. "My mom took my Jeep, and you appear to be car-less."

Landon sets his hands on my shoulders, stepping close enough my mouth goes dry. "Do you have a bike?"

"Yes..."

"What a coincidence. So do I."

"You want to ride our bikes into town?"

Paige and I used to do it all the time—before we got our licenses. Now it seems juvenile.

"Unless you can magically produce a vehicle," he says. "In which case, I will be most impressed."

I shake my head, smiling. There's something different about Landon, something I like. He doesn't care what people think—after all, he'll walk around the camp-ground talking to his camera. Maybe there's freedom in wandering the country, not trying to please the people you see day in and day out.

Landon glances at his video recorder. "Just let me plug this in before we go."

He walks to the door and waves me in. I follow him, hesitant, not wanting to invade his family's space.

"Excuse the mess," he says. "It's somewhat difficult to coexist in such a tight area. Everything tends to go everywhere."

It's not that bad, not really. There's a net for shoes by the door, but a small pair of brown flip-flops—most likely Caleb's—is strewn across the floor. A few dolls, books, and games are scattered on the table. There's a phone charger on the couch next to a half-unzipped hiking backpack.

But other than that, it's pretty tidy.

The family must have George and Candy with them because neither is in the RV—either that or they're sleeping on Mr. and Mrs. Tillman's bed.

A yellow tabby eyes me from her perch on the couch. I'm not sure she's impressed that I've interrupted her nap. Another cat, this one white, watches me from the table cushion. Deciding I'm not the least bit interesting, she begins to groom her face.

"Don't you have a guinea pig in here somewhere?" I ask, looking for a cage.

"In the bunkhouse, on the table under the right-side upper bunk," Landon says absently. "Everyone hates it, but Hunter's attached to the rodent, so it's still traveling with us."

"And the cats get along with it?"

Landon chuckles darkly. "Mostly."

Feeling awkward, I stop in front of a United States map above the dinette. I've seen it before—lots of the people passing through the campground have ones just like it. You add a state sticker for every place you've been.

The Tillmans have been to a lot of states.

Landon catches me staring at it, and he comes to stand by my side. "Crazy, huh?"

"You've been to all those places?" I ask, slightly awed.

Most of the states have stickers, though there are still a few they haven't been to in the middle of the map. Maybe that's what they're doing now—filling in the rest— starting with Colorado.

"We sure have."

I turn to look at him. "In two years?"

He nods. "In two years."

"Wow," I murmur.

For some reason, it makes me sad in a selfish sort of way. Landon's been to all the places I've only read about or seen on TV.

As if sensing the shift in my mood, Landon bumps my shoulder. "The offer still stands—you can hide in our storage compartment when we leave. I'll sneak you trail mix, string cheese, and bottled water."

I laugh. "That's very generous of you."

"I do my best." Remembering our purpose for coming inside, Landon opens a cabinet above the dinette and pulls out a charge cord.

I gape at the equipment he has stored up there. He's like an electronic-hoarding squirrel, hiding away all his cameras, computers, and accessories.

"What could you possibly need all that for?" I ask.

He glances over his shoulder, and a slow, crooked grin builds on his face. "It's for our YouTube channel."

"Your *YouTube channel?*"

Without a word, Landon pulls down a laptop and brings up a page. It takes forever, but it finally loads. And there he is, along with the rest of the Tillmans, staring back at me from the screen. I'm mesmerized both by the content and the fact that their hotspot is working over here.

I step forward and scroll down the page without bothering to ask permission. They have pages and pages of videos...and over a hundred thousand subscribers.

"You're not on there," Landon says casually, hands shoved in his pockets, "if that's what you're worried about. We always ask permission first. I was going to compile the first video before I showed it to you."

I look at him over my shoulder. "This is *yours?*"

"My family's, yeah."

It looks so professional.

"I'm...wow. This is impressive."

Not only are there videos of the United States, but trips to Mexico and Canada as well. The Tillmans have videos of national parks, state parks, theme parks... anything and everything and more. Most have tens of thousands of views, and many of them have even more than that.

"I figured you thought I was insane," he says, "since I talk to my camera all the time."

"Yes, I did."

He laughs, more than a little amused.

"Do you film all these?" I ask.

"No, it's a family effort. But I make about half of them now." Landon gives me another minute to gawk, and then he asks, "Are you ready? I really am starving."

Slowly, I nod and close the laptop, knowing full-well I'm going to stalk the page later tonight.

———

MIDNIGHT ROLLS AROUND, then one, then two. It's three-thirty in the morning right now. I'm going to be worthless when the sun comes up, but I can't seem to close my browser and go to bed. I really do feel like a stalker watching the Tillman's family videos, but it's not like they haven't posted them for all the world to see.

Landon looked younger when they started those two years ago. He was lanky, a little less defined. He didn't talk much in the beginning, was even a bit camera shy. With time, he's gotten bolder, more sure of himself.

He regularly gets mentioned in the comments. *Landon's so cute. Landon's so smart. Landon's so funny.*

I don't love the comment section, to be honest.

Caleb is hilarious, always moving, always questioning, always looking for more. McKenna's darling, and Hunter is...Hunter. He smiles when people aren't looking, is kind and attentive when he doesn't realize the camera is trained on him.

I still can't believe the places they've been, the places they've seen.

Have you watched the one where they went to the Grand Canyon? Paige texts.

I called her last night, filled her in on what I learned. We've been watching them together, from our own homes, and texting each other like we're binge-watching the latest Netflix series.

Yeah, I answer.

I thought Caleb was going to fall off the ledge on that hike!!!

I smile, loving her a little more. She's always there for me, even if it's just to keep me company while I stumble deeper into a crush with a boy I can't have.

There are all kinds of videos on the Tillman's channel—several talking about RV repairs and traveling full time, some explaining the family's favorite meals and how to conserve water and tank space when you're dry camping. I skip a few, but I don't want to miss any with Landon, so I've watched them all for the most part.

Even though it's well into the AM hours, I start another video. They're headed home in this one, meeting with old friends and family. As I watch, the butterflies in my stomach die and are replaced with a chunk of cold, unfeeling iron.

Paige texts several times, but I ignore her, knowing she's seen it too...and I don't want to talk about it.

Half-ill, I end up falling asleep sometime between four and the time my mom comes knocking on my door. Light filters through my curtains, alerting me to the fact that it's morning. My laptop lies next to me, still open.

I blink as Mom pokes her head in the room. I'm so tired my eyes hurt.

"Are you feeling okay?" she asks, frowning.

"I stayed up too late," I admit.

She comes inside and sits on the side of the bed. "What were you doing?"

"Watching YouTube videos," I croak, covering my head with my pillow to block out the light.

"Finally figured out the Tillmans have a channel?"

I peek from below the pillow to glare at her. "You know?"

"Of course I know. Sarah filled me in the day they arrived, explained why they were going to be walking around with cameras and asked if it was okay if they showed some footage of the campground."

I grunt.

"Did you have a good time with Landon yesterday? I saw you go to the cafe for lunch."

Of course she did—the coffee shop is just across the street.

"Yeah."

"It makes me happy to see you having some fun. You work too hard."

"Why does everyone keep saying that?" I demand, pulling the pillow off my face.

"Because you do." She squeezes my shoulder as she stands, heading for the door. "There's banana bread on the counter when you're ready for breakfast. Mark's in the office, and I'm going to sculpt for a while this morning."

"Okay," I mumble, hoping to fall asleep again.

But sleep doesn't come because I learned something last night, something that changes everything.

Landon has a girlfriend.

CHAPTER NINE

SWEATY STRANDS of hair fall in my face, but I ignore them. My whole focus is on the tub in Cabin Three—making sure it's clean, making sure it sparkles.

If I'm not careful, I'll scrub a hole right through the porcelain.

I knew better than to soften my heart to a summer boy.

I knew better.

If I'm hurting, it's my own fault. Summer boys are cheaters. They leave their regular lives, come to Colorado, have flings with the local girls, and then go back to their girlfriends in the fall, pretending nothing happened in the months they were gone.

That's what Thomas did, except he went above and beyond. He cheated on his girlfriend with me, and then he cheated on *me* with *Gia*.

In my mind, Thomas's face blurs with Landon's. They become one and the same—the boy who has a girlfriend back home but shamelessly flirts with the mean-ingless girl he meets on vacation.

"Your mom should give you a raise," a male voice says from behind me. "You're putting a lot of effort into cleaning that crazy-white tub."

Landon.

I whip around, seething mad. "What are *you* doing here?"

His eyes widen with surprise, and he looks torn between responding with shock or laughter. "Your uncle said you were here. I'm going to go out on a limb and guess I've done something to upset you."

I toss the scrub brush in the tub and rip off both of my long, yellow cleaning gloves as I stand. "I watched your videos last night. Straight through."

Slowly, he raises his eyebrows, waiting for me to continue. Something about the fact that he won't even fess up to what he knows I learned irks me even more.

And then the anger leaves me. Like a puff of smoke, it's gone, and I'm left feeling...nothing.

"You have a girlfriend," I say, letting my hands fall to my sides.

He crosses his arms, and his expression grows cool. "You watched the videos chronologically, I assume."

That's how he responds? *Who cares* what order I watched them in?

I hold my hands out—a silent "*so?*"

"You started at the beginning, watched until you saw the footage with Evie, and then you decided I'm a jerk and quit?"

Actually, I fell asleep. I guess I'm a glutton for punishment because before I drifted off, I kept watching, playing video after video until unconsciousness found me.

"We broke up in February." He stares at me, his face unyielding. "It's not something we made a big deal of in the videos, but Hunter mentioned it."

Crossing my arms, mirroring his guarded pose, I study him. His light manner is gone, replaced with something we share. Hurt.

They didn't just break up. Evie left him—I have no doubt.

"I'm sorry," I say, feeling sort of awful—but still a little betrayed, even if it's not justified.

Landon doesn't respond, doesn't even flinch.

"So, what was this?" I motion a hand between us. "From the look on your face, I can tell you're not over her."

Finally, he moves. He looks down and lets out a frustrated breath. "This was me *trying*."

Trying to move on, trying to act normal. I get it. I really do.

The sleepless night catches up with me, and I walk out of the bathroom and sink onto the edge of the bed. "Last summer, a guy started hanging around the campground," I begin, needing to share my own story. "He was cute; he was interesting. He comes to Gray Jay with his family every summer, and I really liked him. We'd been together for two months when I caught him making out with another local girl at a town picnic."

Landon watches me, staying silent.

"I was so hurt," I admit, still feeling a twinge of pain now. "Two weeks later, Thomas's *actual* girlfriend showed up to surprise him for his birthday. It was a surprise all right—she caught him with Gia." I scowl at the comforter. "At least it wasn't me."

"Did you know he had a girlfriend when you were together?"

"No."

Landon's quiet for several long seconds as he processes the information, and then he says, "You are the queen of depressing stories."

I jerk my head his way, meeting his eyes. There's humor there—not much, but a little.

"My mom has been pushing me to 'get back out there,'" Landon says almost wearily.

Slowly, I nod. "Mine too."

"She likes you."

"My mom likes you as well."

He gives me a sideways look. "They've been plotting."

So, he's noticed. The two have been spending all kinds of time together, forming a fast friendship over coffee and sewing projects, apparently plotting ways to "fix" their broken children.

Landon's face softens, and he sits next to me. "How long do you think it will take to get them to leave us alone?"

"About three months, give or take a few weeks."

A morbid smile stretches across his face. "When we leave."

"When you leave," I agree.

He turns his head and studies me. "What if we give them what they want?"

Apparently not all the butterflies are dead because one gives a half-hearted wing wiggle in my stomach. "What?"

"Be my girlfriend, just for the summer. If they think we're together, they'll dream up another project and leave us alone."

"Like...fake girlfriend?"

It sounds lame...but it's not entirely ridiculous.

"It wouldn't be a terrible thing to have you by my side when Thomas shows up," I muse out loud as I run an appraising eye over him. Not terrible at all.

Landon laughs—it's a real laugh too, not a morbid one. "I'm nearly positive Evie still watches our channel."

I picture her—this ex-girlfriend. I'm sure she's pretty. Guys like Landon don't usually date girls who aren't.

I'm quiet for too long, and he looks over.

"You're a little too charming for a fake girlfriend," I say. "Why don't you find yourself a real one?"

"I don't have the energy for a real one." He tilts his head to the side. "Why don't you find a real boyfriend to throw in Thomas's face?"

"I don't have the patience for one," I answer.

"Fair enough." He holds out his hand. "So, how about it? Real friends, fake dating?"

I study him for several moments, and then I clasp my palm in his. "Yeah. Okay."

———

HAND IN HAND, Landon and I walk into the coffee shop. Mom's not here today, but since Betta sells her art, they talk often. It won't take long for news of my date with Landon to reach her.

The bell tinkles over the door as we walk inside, and people glance our way. It's packed for mid-afternoon, but I only recognize a few locals. It's usually nothing but tourists this time of year.

"Hey, Betta," I call, stepping up to the counter. The owner is about the same age as my mom, but her brunette hair grayed early. She chose to go the natural route, and she wears her almost white locks long and usually twisted up. She's the organic, natural type, though I know for a fact she visits the pizza place every Friday evening with her niece for a deluxe pepperoni with extra cheese.

Betta's eyes go between Landon and me, and a big smile lights her face. "Good afternoon, Lacey. You haven't been in for a while."

"We've been busy," I tell her.

She shakes her head as she puts the finishing touches on a latte she's working on. "Your mom says you work too much."

I roll my eyes. "I've heard."

Laughing, Betta hands the latte to the waiting patron

and turns her full attention to us. She smiles at Landon. "And who might you be?"

Even though Landon isn't a real boyfriend, I still feel my cheeks heating. This is what it's like in a small town—everywhere you go, it's like bringing a boy home to meet your parents.

"I'm Landon," my incredibly good-looking, faux boyfriend says, giving Betta a smile.

Properly charmed, she laughs like she's happy to make his acquaintance, but I know she's *actually* delighted for new gossip. "Well, it's a pleasure to meet you, Landon. Are you staying in Gray Jay long?"

I freeze as Landon casually drapes his arm over my shoulder, pulling me to his side like an affectionate boyfriend would. He gives me a squeeze, reminding me to play along. The problem is that I'm trying not to swoon.

He doesn't need to know that though.

Betta nods as Landon tells her about his family's summer plans, and I stand next to him, trying not to breathe in the clean scent of his deodorant. *Who does that?*

Another couple steps up behind us, and Betta realizes she better get back to work. "What can I get you two?"

We order, and then Landon pays before I can stop him.

"Why did you do that?" I hiss while we're waiting for Betta to make the drinks.

"Because we're *dating*," he whispers back.

"I'll pay you back," I whisper.

He flashes me a flirtatious smile. "Don't worry about it. I got it."

If he keeps looking at me like that, I'm going to forget this is a ruse.

Betta hands us our drinks after a few minutes and commands us to go enjoy the sunshine while it lasts.

Landon holds the door for me as we leave the coffee shop, and then we amble down the road, sipping our drinks.

"Busy place," Landon says. "Does she handle it all by herself?"

"Paige and a few other kids from school help out when she needs it. My mom steps in every once in a while too."

"Doesn't your mom have her hands full with the campground?"

"Yes, but it gives her a chance to talk to the people who ask about her sculptures in person. She enjoys it."

"Can I ask you something?" he says after another long moment.

I nod.

"Where's your dad? You mentioned him at the falls, but I didn't want to pry."

The question doesn't sting anymore, not like it did when I was little, but I miss him, miss the *idea* of him. Things would be so different if he were still alive.

"He passed away when I was six. He had a rare form of pancreatic cancer."

"I'm sorry," Landon says, at a loss for words, as most people are when they first learn.

I tap his arm. "It's okay—I'm okay."

"So, your uncle came to live with you after that?"

"Yep. Mom couldn't manage the campground and take care of me at the same time, so she was going to have to sell. Uncle Mark knew how much it meant to her and Dad, so he stepped in, started taking care of both of us."

"And he's your mom's brother?"

"Dad's brother."

People don't always know what to say to that at first. They jump to conclusions, assume that Mark and Mom's relationship is romantic because Mark moved all the way to Colorado to help Mom out after Dad died. But it's not like that. It would be weird if it were.

Mark's become like a father to me, but he thinks of Mom as a sister, nothing more. We're a strange little family—but a family all the same.

Landon says something else, but I don't know what because I spy someone on the street I'd rather avoid.

"Let's go this way—" I begin, already nudging Landon down a quaint, vegetable-garden-lined alley. But I'm too late.

"Lacey!" a girl calls in greeting, waving her hand to make sure I don't miss her.

I growl under my breath, and though I think I'm quiet, Landon turns his head like he heard it. "Friend of yours?" he asks, saying "friend" in a questioning way.

The girl trots toward us, making her long braid bounce back and forth. She's super short, barely five-foot, and her hair is naturally the shade of platinum blond the Hollywood types would kill for.

"Hey, Gia," I say, working up a smile.

Landon's lips part with understanding when he hears the name, but he doesn't let on that we've talked about the home-wrecker before.

Gia stops in front of us, catching her breath. "I haven't seen you in forever!"

She looks cute today, as usual, in short leggings, a jersey skirt, and a tank top that it's not quite warm enough for. She's always reminded me of those eighteen-inch dolls I used to play with—the quintessential girl next door...except she's got curves in places those sorts of dolls don't usually have.

She rocks an innocent yet flirty vibe that a lot of guys can't get enough of, and I wasn't ready for Landon to meet her. He's only fake-dating me— nothing is keeping him from real-dating *her*. And the thought of Landon with Gia is enough to make my blood boil.

"I'm Gia," she says, clasping his hand, holding it for a second longer than she should before she releases it.

"Landon," my fake boyfriend says with a nod.

She eyes him, giving him a come-hither look that unsuspecting guys might misconstrue as friendly when it's actually predatory. "Are you staying in Gray Jay?"

"At Lacey's place," Landon says. Then, smooth as ever, he wraps his arm around my back, resting his hand on the curve of my waist and pulling me to his side.

A little nervous Gia's going to see right through the charade, I almost let out a slightly hysteric giggle. His hand is right above my hip, warm through the thin fabric of my T-shirt, and it's making my mind wander in directions it has no right going.

I'm so preoccupied, I don't register the next several moments of the conversation until Gia says, "So you'll come?"

I stiffen. "Where?"

She laughs at my absentmindedness and tosses her braid over her shoulder. "To my great aunt's house next Friday."

Oh, no.

Misty Maguire's teen nights are the lamest thing ever. The woman isn't a day under eighty years old. Occasionally, she gets the wild idea to invite all the local teens and gives them free run of the big white barn on her property. She picks out a movie, creates a *theme* to go along with it, and shows it with a big projector on the side of the building.

The problem is, most of the movies are more age-appropriate for kids around Caleb and McKenna's ages. Most of the couples end up sneaking into the barn to find a private corner of the hayloft, leaving the rest of us to drink juice boxes and silently bemoan our single status.

Yet all the local kids go because it's impossible to have a social life here, and we're that desperate for entertainment. But it's not an event you bring summer boys to— not unless you're trying to scare them away.

"Sounds great," Landon says.

For just a second, Gia's eyes flicker to the hand

holding me close, and she frowns. Then she brightens again and gives us—more Landon than me—a big smile.

"Great!" she chirps and then holds up the shopping bag at her side. "I have to get back, but I'll see you there."

We say our goodbyes, and I watch her leave, my eyes narrowed and an uneasy feeling in the pit of my stomach.

"So, that's Gia, huh?" Landon asks, his arm still wrapped around my back.

"Yeah."

"The one who stole your last boyfriend?" He says it with a teasing glint in his eyes—a sweet, affectionate glint I find most confusing.

"Yeah."

He tugs me tight one last time before he lets me go. Then, lightly, just before taking a sip of his rapidly melting iced coffee, he says, "Well, no worries. She won't steal me."

CHAPTER TEN

I'M in the middle of cutting up chicken for dinner when my phone rings. Though I'm unable to answer, I glance at the screen to see who it is. For a moment, my stomach flutters with the hope that it might be Landon. Which is ridiculous because we haven't exchanged numbers and we're not actually dating—something it seems I must remind myself continually.

Seeing that it's Paige, I go back to the cutting board to finish before I call her back. I'm slicing the last piece when she calls again.

It must be important because she's not usually this needy. I dump the chicken cubes into the hot skillet and hurry to wash my hands.

Quickly, I answer her call, only to realize I was a moment too late. I dial her number, starting to worry there's some kind of emergency.

"You're dating Landon?" she demands the moment

she answers the phone. "And what the heck, Lacey? I found out from *Gia*."

I almost laugh with relief that she's not sick or dying in a hole somewhere, and then I step onto the back porch where I hope my mom won't hear me. "We're not actually dating. We're just making people think we're together so our mothers will quit playing Team Matchmaker."

She's quiet for a second as she processes it. Then, apparently confused, she asks, "Why don't you just date him for real? Even if you won't admit it, I know you like him."

Sighing, I sit on the swinging bench. "He just broke up with his girlfriend a few months ago, and he's not over her. And I don't date summer guys anymore—you know that."

"Yeah, but it's a stupid rule. You can't assume every guy is like Thomas."

I know she's right, but it's not that easy.

"I saw him yesterday," she says, her tone too casual.

"Who?" I ask, but I already know.

"Thomas."

"His family's back then? At Upper Ridge?"

"Yep." She pauses. "There's a girl with him. Gia thinks she's the girlfriend."

Surely it's not the same one.

Guilt cloaks me. I really didn't know Thomas had a girlfriend when I was dating him. For obvious reasons, he didn't inform me. But I still feel like a cow.

"What were you doing at Upper Ridge?" I ask,

changing the subject. "Traitor."

She laughs, and it's a tinkling, happy sound. "Tanner asked me out."

Poor Jarrett, I think.

"So, you went out with him last night?" I ask, going inside to stir the chicken before it burns.

"Yes, and it was amazing," she gushes.

Properly distracted, she goes on about her date for the next fifteen minutes. Every time it seems like she's going to return to the subject of Landon and me, I steer her away. I don't want her dissecting my feelings for him.

"Are you going to Misty's thing next Friday?" I ask when dinner is just about finished.

"She's planned one already?" Paige groans. "Summer just started."

"Yep, and thanks to Gia, Landon and I are going."

"I'll bring Tanner," she says. "We'll make it fun."

Then she suddenly laughs like she's just thought of something.

"What?" I ask, nervous.

"You're going to have to take Landon into the barn, or no one will believe you're actually dating."

My chest tightens, and my stomach grows warm. "The only one I have to convince is my mom."

"You know how gossip spreads in this town. But if you don't want to make it believable..."

"You are such a brat."

I can practically hear her grin. "I know, but you love me anyway."

I growl, reluctantly agreeing, and then we end the

call.

"Who was that?" Mom asks, startling me as she walks into the kitchen.

"Paige." I flash her a guilty look, hoping she didn't overhear that last part.

Oblivious, she fills glasses with ice and puts the silverware on the table. "What do you need to convince me of?"

Crud.

I dish the chicken pasta onto three plates and set them on the table. "To let me go to Misty's for her teen night next Friday."

"Why couldn't you go?"

Suddenly, I realize my out. "Because of our s'mores bonfire! That's my evening to host it."

She waves her hand like it's no big deal. "I'll take care of it. Go ahead."

Well, drat.

"I'll do tomorrow's bonfire," I offer, feeling guilty for pawning off my night on her.

"If you want."

Uncle Mark comes in, thankfully announcing there's an electrical post that needs replacing, and he and Mom begin a conversation about updating all the electrical in A Loop.

I'm quiet through dinner, but neither of them notices. Though I don't want it to, my mind wanders to Landon, next Friday night, and Misty's hayloft.

———

"DON'T FEED THAT TO CANDY," Hunter tells his sister in the snottiest voice imaginable.

McKenna glares at him as she takes a bite of her ooey, gooey, I-can't-believe-she-used-two-roasted-marshmallows-on-that-thing s'more. Chocolate and marshmallow squish out from between the graham crackers, threatening to make a sticky mess.

"Hunter," Mrs. Tillman says in the universal mom voice that basically means stop talking immediately or you're grounded.

The sun only set about fifteen minutes ago, and it's the most pleasant time of the day—still warm, but just starting too cool off for the evening. Since I traded with Mom, it's my night to host the Friday night bonfire, and my fire is puny. The small crowd doesn't seem to mind though.

We're gathered near the gazebo, in the area Uncle Mark built years ago just for this. He crafted long seats from four massive logs, and they make a square around the huge, brick fire ring.

Tonight, we don't just have families with kids. Mr. and Mrs. Murray are here with Todd, the fancy-pedigreed golden retriever. Greg and Hallie Hendrick, the couple I initially mistook Landon's parents for, brought their Greyhound, Bark, with them as well.

And of course, McKenna brought Candy. Tonight, the cotton ball is stuffed into a red and black checkered vest, the kind that screams iconic camper. To top off the outfit, Candy wears her usual diamond-rhinestone-studded collar. It's a Barbie-goes-camping, canine fashionista kind of style, and it's obvious Candy thinks she's pretty hot stuff. She won't even give the other dogs the time of day, and they want to play with her so badly.

"He's really well-behaved," I say to Greg and Hallie when Bark noses my leg, wanting attention.

"He's the best dog," Greg answers. "Even if he has terrible separation anxiety."

"What do you do when you have to go grocery shopping?" I ask. "Or sight-seeing where dogs aren't allowed?"

Greg scratches the dog's shoulder. "He has a crate that he feels safe in, and we give him toys. He does all right as long as we're not gone too long."

Mrs. Murray ends up continuing the conversation, asking about Bark's lineage. Apparently, he's a retired racer. He's about nine now, so he can't move like he used to, but back when he was young, before the Hendricks adopted him, he was a champion.

"Where's George?" I ask Landon as he plays the part of my doting boyfriend and offers to roast a marshmallow for me. It's too early—we should really wait until the fire dies down and the coals are glowing, but the kids hate waiting, and so do I.

Landon kneels by the fire. "He's scared of the dark—we leave him in the camper at night because otherwise, he'll refuse to move, and you have to drag him."

"But he's huge," I say with a laugh. "What's out there that he could possibly be afraid of?"

Flashing me a smile over his shoulder, Landon shrugs. A few minutes later, he stands, offering me the perfectly browned marshmallow.

"Impressive," I say.

He gives me a crooked grin and leans a smidgen closer. "I've had some practice."

I realize he's playing it up for his family, but for some reason, my breath catches. I glance toward Mrs. Tillman, self-conscious. A part of me, a teeny-tiny part, feels kind of guilty. She just wants Landon to be happy, and we're lying to them.

What's she going to think about me when she finds out we were never together?

"Make me one next!" Caleb begs Landon.

"You're already roasting one," I point out.

Landon's little brother gives me a look. "I'm *burning* this one."

"Don't waste other people's marshmallows," Mrs. Tillman says.

Caleb's face falls. And why wouldn't it? What kid doesn't love watching a white, fluffy marshmallow turn into a torch? It's the only time you're actually allowed to play with fire.

"We don't care," I assure Landon's mom.

She purses her lips and then shrugs, giving him permission. A few moments later, Caleb's wielding an impressive flaming marshmallow.

"Look!" he exclaims, so excited he ends up whirling around, taking the mass of burning sugar goo with him.

"Keep it over the fire!" Mr. Tillman commands. "And don't *shake* it."

For some reason, Landon's mom looks a touch nervous. Even Bark moves away from the boy.

"Can I have another s'more?" McKenna asks through the final bite of her first one.

"No," Mr. and Mrs. Tillman say at the same time.

McKenna pouts for several seconds, and then she turns to Hallie Hendrick. "Did you know Irish Wolfhounds are the tallest dogs? They're even bigger than Great Danes, though there was a Great Dane that was taller than any other dog *ever*."

Hallie's about five years older than I am—maybe twenty-two, twenty-three—and kind of quiet. But she has a kind smile, so I think she's nice enough—just shy. She brushes her chin-length, light brunette hair behind her ear and says, "I did know that. Did you know English commoners were forbidden from owning Greyhounds in medieval times?"

Finding a kindred spirit, McKenna moves next to Hallie and starts an in-depth conversation about dogs. The girl pets Bark, making Candy jealous. Not about to be ignored, the tiny dog makes friends with the Greyhound. Soon the two are playing—well, Candy plays. Bark lies on the ground and paws at her as she jumps around him.

Caleb's burning marshmallow finally turns black and falls into the fire to join the coals, and Landon roasts him a proper one. A few more families join us, and the sky darkens to velvety indigo.

It gets cold as the light fades. I forgot to grab a jacket before I left the house, so I hug myself, rubbing my arms to keep warm.

"Are you cold?" Landon asks, already shrugging off his sweatshirt.

"I'm fine," I say, and then I shiver.

"Take it," he coaxes and holds the sweatshirt out.

He's playing the part. Or maybe he's just genuinely nice and cares that I'm frozen. It's not because he necessarily *wants* me to wear his sweatshirt.

"Thanks." I take it and pull it over my head, realizing my mistake immediately. Soapy, wonderful, Landon-ness surrounds me, making me want to melt, just like one of his perfectly toasted marshmallows. The fabric is still warm, too.

Then, just to top it off, Landon wraps his arms around my middle and pulls my back to his chest, blocking the chill. I feel like a sparking live wire, but Landon's all loose and relaxed.

He should go into acting—he really should.

I rest my head back because I would be a fool to pass up this kind of opportunity. Landon shifts, tugging me closer, and sets his chin on top of my head. I've never dated someone tall enough to do that.

Or *not* dated...

"Ew," Hunter mutters, rolling his eyes.

Mr. Tillman tosses a marshmallow at his surly son.

"Don't waste the marshmallows!" Mrs. Tillman exclaims, exasperated.

I'd assure her again we couldn't care less, but I'm practically floating above the fire, not capable of simple conversation.

And though I don't mean to—or even want to—my

brain can't help but compare Landon to Thomas. It's nothing major, just little things, like the way it feels to be in Landon's arms, how tall he is, the way his sweatshirt feels and smells.

It hits me that I don't remember those small things about Thomas as well as I thought I did. He never lent me his sweatshirt or a jacket. I don't even remember what it's like to kiss him, not really.

Naturally, *that* thought leads to an imagined scene in Misty's hayloft involving Landon—a place that's marked with metaphorical flashing warning lights and bright yellow tape. We can't go there. And I'm sure Landon doesn't want to—not with the breakup still so fresh in his mind.

Do I want to though?

No.

No.

Maybe?

It doesn't matter.

"Do you care if I film a bit for the vlog?" Mr. Tillman asks.

I freeze, and I'm afraid Landon can tell.

"We don't have to," Landon says quietly.

I shake my head. "No, it's all right."

Mr. Tillman asks the rest of the guests, and they all agree. From my cozy spot in Landon's arms, I smile for the camera, feeling like a fraud. All the while I'm wishing, maybe just a little bit, that we weren't just pretending.

CHAPTER ELEVEN

AFTER STARING at my closet for far too long, I end up in a pair of jeans, a cute, blousy top, and a pair of impractical ballet flats that I rarely wear.

Because the night is casual, I've pulled my hair up in a high ponytail again and curled the ends. Hopefully, I won't get hay caught in it.

Don't go there.

Thoughts of kissing Landon in the hayloft have consumed my week. This morning, I poured salt in my coffee. It tasted so awful, I ended up spitting it across the table. Mom looked at me like I sprouted another head and asked if I stayed up all night watching videos again.

The doorbell rings, pulling me from my thoughts. I'm so edgy, I almost hide in my closet. I can't do this.

I hear the front door open, and Mom greets Landon.

"Lacey," she calls after a few moments. "Landon's here."

Standing tall, I give myself a silent pep talk in the mirror. It's going to be okay. It's just a lame party.

I walk into the living room, trying not to think about how much this feels like a date—a real date. Landon smiles when he sees me, and my breath catches. He's lounging against the doorjamb, arms loosely crossed, making small talk with my mother.

"Ready?" Landon asks.

"Yep." Thankfully, no one seems to notice the fake cheer in my voice.

"Have fun!" Mom says, clasping her hands and watching us with wide, happy eyes. Her enthusiasm doesn't make the situation any less awkward.

Landon jiggles a pair of keys when we step out the door. "I actually get to drive you somewhere."

The Tillman's Suburban is parked right next to my Jeep in all its shining, brand-new glory. Landon opens my door and flashes me a smile that makes my stomach flutter.

Not a date. Not a date. Not a date.

Landon, however, doesn't seem uncomfortable. He effortlessly keeps up the conversation as he navigates down the winding mountain roads, taking turns as I direct him.

We pull onto Misty's drive in about twenty minutes. Judging from the number of people outside, we arrived neither too early or too late. Every pair of eyes latches onto the Suburban as Landon parks.

Hoping Landon doesn't notice, I take a deep, calming breath, preparing myself for the inquisition. I know these kids, grew up with most of them. They'll see right through me.

I open my door, but Landon meets me before I hop out. Leaning close, he sets his hand on either side of my waist and quietly says, "It's going to be fine."

Our eyes meet, and I wonder if I should lean in and kiss him for the sake of appearances. The thought makes me warm, fluttery.

As if reading my mind, Landon's eyes drop to my lips. I hold my breath, waiting...hoping.

After a moment, he swallows and shifts back, giving me space to think. He takes my hand the moment I close the door, and we amble toward our hawk-eyed spectators. They hastily continue their conversations, only shooting us sideways glances, pretending they weren't gawking a moment ago.

Paige appears, and she pulls me into a greeting embrace. Softly, so only I will hear, she says, "Oh. My. Wow. What was *that?*"

"Too much?" I ask, breaking away as Jarrett introduces himself to Landon.

"Don't even pretend that was a show," she murmurs, smiling as she turns to the group that's joined us. Tanner extends his arms, and she steps into them, practically purring.

Jarrett glances at them for only a moment before he looks back at Landon. He's doing a decent job pretending it doesn't bother him that his cousin is dating Paige, but I can tell from his tight expression, it does.

I glance around, noticing the music, and turn to Paige. "Where's the movie?"

"Apparently Gia suggested we just do music this time. Misty actually went with it." She widens her eyes, showing her incredulous shock.

"So...no kid movie?" I ask, starting to panic. Cartoon bunnies were the only thing keeping this faux date from feeling a little too appealing.

"No kid movie," Paige confirms.

"Where's Misty?"

"In the house. Her only rule is no alcohol or 'being stupid,' which I guess she figures covers a whole array of things."

"Fun things," Tanner says, nuzzling Paige's neck.

She giggles, and I look away, slightly repulsed. I don't know if I dislike Tanner, or if I just don't like him with Paige.

Or maybe all these years, I've been rooting for Jarrett.

The two laugh about something, and then Tanner tugs my friend away, leaving us so they can mingle. I shake my head as they disappear and scan the party.

There's only about thirty of us, ages ranging from about sixteen to twenty. There are only a few faces I don't recognize. Besides the local kids, visiting cousins mill about—regulars who we see every year. Though the group is small, it's still a good turnout for one of Misty's parties. Word must have gotten around that Gia somehow managed to veto the movie.

The sun sinks behind the mountains, but the perimeter of tiki lights circling the front of the barn does a decent job of keeping the mosquitos and gnats away. Someone turns up the music, and people begin to dance, which seems odd.

Dancing is usually relegated to school functions with a neighboring high school in the next county, and it takes place in a stale-smelling gym, not surrounded by firelight under a blanket of stars.

Without the singing cartoon animals and princess-themed cookies, Misty's acreage is proving to be a rather romantic setting.

"Come on," Landon says, taking my hand.

I let him guide me into the small throng of people, hoping my discomfort doesn't show. When he stops, I step into him and let my hands loop around his neck, school-dance style. Though it seems weird to dance in jeans and a T-shirt, it's somehow better, more impromptu.

"I don't suppose you went to many dances?" I ask him, hoping to fill the limited space between us with small talk.

"I managed to make several, actually." He moves his hands from my sides and clasps them behind my back. The move nudges us closer, but in a sweet way, like an extended embrace. I want to bury my nose against his T-shirt, breathe in the clean scent of laundry detergent and the smell of his soap.

"We made it back home for homecoming both my junior and senior year," he continues, watching me carefully. "But prom just my junior year."

He's telling me something, something he doesn't want to say with words.

My stomach drops when I realize why it was important he went back—it was because of his girlfriend.

"How long were you and Evie together?" I ask, moving my gaze to his shoulder when the eye contact becomes too uncomfortable.

"Three years."

"Three years?"

He laughs, but it's not a raw sound as I might expect. "We were next-door neighbors, grew up together."

I want to groan—neighbors? Practically in love since they were children? How am I supposed to compete with that?

Wait—no.

There is no competition. *This isn't real.*

Landon looks up at the sky. "We fought all the time. I always thought it was chemistry—you know, *passion*." He rolls his eyes. "But in truth, it was nothing but exhausting."

The passion part makes my skin crawl, even though he says the word in a scoffing voice, but I try to hide my revulsion for Landon's sake.

"She ended up cheating on me before we broke up," he says softly. "Gave me the *"it's me, not you"* line when I found out."

I meet his eyes, understanding completely. It's a horrible thing to be cheated on, makes you feel like you're meaningless. Trivial.

"Enough about Evie," he says, rolling his shoulders,

physically shaking off the somber mood. "The last thing I want to do is talk about the guy you dated, so I doubt you want to hear about her."

Over his shoulder, Gia pulls someone into the center of the party. "*Thomas.*"

Landon nods. "Yeah."

I stare at the boy standing next to Gia, and a cold, slimy feeling settles in my stomach. Hearing about Landon's ex-girlfriend is bad, but it's nothing compared to this.

"No," I say, pulling my gaze from Gia to meet Landon's eyes. Then I nod to the side, directing his attention to the table of refreshments that Misty provided. "He's *here.*"

CHAPTER TWELVE

"IS THAT HIM?" Landon asks, almost as surprised as I am. Almost.

"Yeah," I focus on Landon's shirt though all I want to do is run back to the Suburban, beg him to take me home.

I knew I'd have to face him again, but I wasn't ready. I don't know if I'd ever be ready.

"What's he doing?" I hiss at a whisper. "Has he spotted me? How does he look?"

"He looks short," Landon says mildly, readjusting his hold on me.

"You know what I mean." I give Landon a rueful look. "And besides, you're at least six two. Most everyone is short compared to you."

Landon's lips quirk in a wicked half-smile. "Six-two *and a half.*"

"And proud of it," I tease, though my heart isn't into the playful banter at the moment. I peek at Thomas, trying not to be obvious about it.

"Hey, Lacey?" Landon asks.

"Yeah?" I probably sound distracted because I'm searching for Thomas's girlfriend. According to Paige, she's supposed to be in Gray Jay too.

Landon waits before continuing, apparently wanting me to look his way. Feeling his eyes on me, I finally give in and transfer all my attention to him.

He leans close. With his breath tickling my jaw, he asks, "Do you want me to kiss you? To make him jealous?"

I open my mouth to say something—I have no idea *what*—when Landon winds a hand through my ponytail, caressing his fingers against my neck in the process.

"O...okay," I finally manage.

It's a show—I know that, but I find myself forgetting about Thomas. Landon moves closer, tilting his head, his eyes locked on mine. His breath is fresh, minty, and I absently wonder if he planned this.

My stomach tightens at the thought, and my pulse jumps.

"How's this?" Landon whispers just as his lips tease mine.

"Fine," I murmur.

"Do you think he's noticed?" Landon's free hand is on my waist, nudging me closer but giving me the freedom to step away. But I don't want to step away.

I shift closer, mimicking Landon's unhurried approach even though every inch of me tingles with anticipation.

Still, he doesn't kiss me, not yet.

"Well?" I ask, my voice more breathy than impatient. "Are you going to kiss me or not?"

Landon groans, and his fingers gently dig into my sides. It's a soft sound of restraint, but it lights a fire in my chest, makes me want more. I breathe in his clean scent, forgetting about the people around us, focused only on Landon and his hands and lips and mouth.

Kiss me already.

"Lacey!" Gia calls, her voice as sweet as syrup.

I close my eyes, loathing her more than I ever have in my life—which is saying something.

With a small smile—perhaps even a *frustrated* smile— Landon pulls back and turns to Gia and Thomas. He keeps me close, gently tugging me to his side, and he wraps a sweetly possessive hand above my hip. The move is so perfectly executed; *I* almost believe we're together.

This is a dangerous ruse.

"Thomas," I say, working up a great big fake smile. "Hey."

He and Gia walk our way. My ex looks decidedly uncomfortable, which I rather like. But even though we didn't part on good terms, I'm willing to pretend it's all water under the bridge if he is...which is a lot easier to do with Landon's arm wrapped around me.

"This is Landon," I say.

Landon gives Thomas a cool nod—not rude in any way, but not exactly friendly either.

Gia shifts her weight, eyeing Thomas. What's she doing with him? He played her just as much as he did his girlfriend and me. Maybe it's easy to be quick to leap back in when your heart was never involved—and judging by how quickly she started dating after Thomas left, I think it's a safe bet to say her heart never had anything to do with it.

If she has one. Which I'm not convinced she does.

"So, you're back," I say to break the uncomfortable silence that falls over us like a thick, fleecy blanket of awkwardness.

Thomas looks exactly as I remember him—dark hair, fair skin, delicate complexion that makes him appear aristocratic and a bit haughty. He's striking.

But now I see him through Landon's eyes, and I'm noticing things for the first time. He is sort of short—only a few inches taller than I am. His blue eyes are pretty, but they're usually scrunched in a way that makes you wonder if he's looking down on the whole world.

It's obvious he thinks Misty's party is below him, so I have no idea why he decided to show up.

"Every year," he answers, crossing his arms, studying me. "How are you?"

I give him the usual spiel—work's good. Mom and Mark are fine.

"Where's your girlfriend?" I eventually ask, tired of the small talk. If the question makes him uncomfortable, so be it. Maybe he'll leave, and Landon and I can get back to...whatever Landon and I were doing. "I look forward to meeting her."

"I don't have a girlfriend," Thomas says. At least he has the decency to look embarrassed. "Haven't for a long time."

A long time? About ten months? Maybe when she surprised him during his summer vacation and found out he'd been cheating on her?

But what about the girl Paige said Gia saw him with?

The question burns in my stomach like an ulcer, but I don't dare ask.

Gia tucks herself against Thomas's side, staking a claim on a boy I don't want. "His *cousin* Leia is with them this year," she says.

Yep, that explains it.

The message Gia sends is unspoken but loud and clear—Thomas is single, and she wants him. Well, that's peachy. She's welcome to him.

"Sounds fun," I say, unwrapping myself from Landon's patient arms and taking his hand. "Well, have a good time."

Landon follows, no questions asked.

"Lacey..." Thomas calls and then trails off, probably unsure what to say. Maybe it should go a little something like this: *"I'm sorry I used you to cheat on my girlfriend and then started cheating on the both of you with Gia."*

It's the kind of thing you have to say in person because they just don't make greeting cards for that sort of apology.

Without waiting for Thomas to get his thoughts in order, I give the pair a curt, indifferent wave and pull Landon into the barn.

"Where are we going?" he asks, lowering his voice as if the darkened atmosphere means we should whisper.

"Away from them."

I cried countless tears over Thomas. I imagined our first meeting all this time—looked forward to it with equal amounts of dread and eagerness—and pictured all the things I would say and do. But actually seeing him again was somehow anticlimactic, unmemorable even.

With Landon obediently trailing behind me, I climb the ladder to the hayloft. It's not completely dark. Firelight from the tiki torches shines in through the large front window, which is open to the night. I glance around to see if anyone is up here, but it looks like we have the loft to ourselves.

As soon as Landon's up the ladder, I sit on a bale, waiting for him to join me. Even though it's been haunting my thoughts all week, I didn't bring Landon here for the same reason other couples find the space so appealing. I came to escape.

Outside, the music gets even louder, which convinces me that I made the right decision. I don't feel like being fun and social—that's Paige's thing, not mine.

"There's actually hay up here," Landon says, sounding bemused by the quaintness of it.

"Technically, this is straw."

Landon sits beside me. "Are there mice?"

"Scared?" I tease him, though he doesn't sound nervous. I scoot closer to bump his shoulder—or maybe I scoot closer just to be closer. "Misty has lots of cats prowling the property. I think we're safe."

He turns his head, meeting my eyes in the dark. Though I can't see him well, I can tell he's smiling that crooked smile of his, the one that makes my knees weak.

"I, too, will protect you from tiny rodents should the need arise."

"That's very brave of you," I say with a laugh, and then I look down at my hands, which I've clasped on my lap. "Thank you. It was much easier facing him for the first time with you there."

Landon only nods—maybe he doesn't know what to say. This is a weird situation we've gotten ourselves into. We say we're fake dating, but I'm genuinely attracted to him, and I think there's a chance he likes me too. My mind wanders to our almost-kiss, and my pulse quickens. We're alone, entirely by ourselves. There's no reason to kiss him now, not when it won't help convince people of our ruse. But I want to.

Oh, I want to.

"Do you think we were believable?" Landon asks.

"Hmmm?" My eyes are focused on the lack of space between us, on Landon's arm pressed next to mine as we share the bale of straw.

From the corner of my eye, I see Landon look my way. "Do you think we were believable? As a couple?"

Slowly, I look up. Our eyes meet, and my stomach tightens. "I think so."

His expression is enigmatic in the dark—I have no idea what he's thinking, but I know what I'm *feeling*. There's an invisible cord between us, drawing us together.

He waits another moment before he says, "Maybe we should practice."

I think he means to say the words playfully, but

there's a dark catch in his voice that tunnels under my defenses. It makes me forget all the sound reasons why I stay away from summer boys, especially ones as tempting as Landon.

"Probably," I find myself answering, even though a tiny, still-sane part of my brain screams warnings at me, desperately hoping I'll listen.

But I push those warnings away, smother them while dwelling on sensations instead—the feel of the cold mountain air surrounding us, the flickering firelight, the fresh scent of Landon's cotton shirt blending with the smell of the straw.

"For the sake of credibility," he murmurs. We're close enough his words tickle my lips.

Fully distracted by his mouth, I nod. "Absolutely."

We wait for the other to change their mind, to back down from the unspoken dare. So much more in tune with my senses in the dark, I can feel my heartbeat, hear each breath Landon takes.

Several moments go by, then a few more.

And then, when I think I will simply die if he changes his mind, he wraps a warm hand around the back of my neck, and our mouths meet.

It's a testing kiss, the tentative kind that starts slow but builds until it takes your breath away and makes you forget your own name. Landon's lips are firm, soft, *perfect*. I angle toward him, tossing my leg over the straw bale to straddle it and reach him better. His hands settle at my waist, a warm contrast to the cool night, and he pulls me closer still.

For several moments, I forget that we're pretending—I forget about Thomas and Gia and worrying over Paige. There's nothing but Landon and the dusky light.

Only voices from below could interrupt the single-minded bliss that is kissing Landon. The two of us freeze, lips only a breath apart, listening. His spearmint-scented breath fills the space between us, and I want nothing more than to meet him once again.

But there's an abrupt giggle and the sound of shuffling as someone—or maybe two *someones*—climb the ladder.

CHAPTER THIRTEEN

I SET a single finger over Landon's lips, alerting him to be quiet, and then I take his hand and creep from the bale, farther into the darkened corner. There's more straw here, stacked up three high, but next to the wall, there's a gap with just enough room for two people to sit in reasonable comfort.

Gia's whispered voice fills the hayloft, and then Thomas's joins her. I tense, and the warm, languid feeling fades and is replaced with dead, impartial irritation.

"He's doing it on purpose to get a rise out of you," Landon whispers, his lips next to my ear so Gia and Thomas won't overhear. Then he wraps his arms around my middle and tugs my back against his chest, holding me tightly. The move is comforting. The spark between us has faded to a companionable simmer. "Ignore them. We'll sneak out as soon as we can."

I close my eyes and lean into him, trying to pretend we're alone again.

Suddenly, the music comes to an abrupt stop. I hear several raised voices, one of which I'm positive is Misty's.

"What's going on out there?" I hear Gia ask Thomas. He's just answering when the overhead lights flip on, washing the barn in a harsh fluorescent glow.

I shrink further into our straw-bale-surrounded cubby. Beside me, Landon does the same. We're mostly hidden, even in the light, but we don't dare move.

The old ladder creaks and groans as Misty climbs up it, muttering under her breath.

"Gia," she says, her voice hard. I can almost picture her with her hands on her hips and a hard scowl on her softly wrinkled face. "Just what do you think the two of you are doing up here in the dark?"

Gia, obviously nervous, lets out a sharp giggle.

"Go on," Misty says. "Party's over."

Landon and I stay still and hidden as the three leave the hayloft. Their footsteps echo as they walk across the wooden floor below, and then it's silent.

"We should probably get going too," Landon says, inadvertently whispering the words across the back of my neck.

I shiver. "Yeah."

He stands and helps me to my feet. We manage to sneak from the barn without anyone noticing and slip into Landon's Suburban just as the last few stragglers are leaving.

Landon's quiet, but so am I.

I wonder if some part of him feels guilty for kissing me. Maybe he feels like he cheated on the girl he's not with anymore. Part of me feels guilty as well, but not because of Thomas. No—it's not that. It's because I can feel my convictions slipping away. My protective walls are crumbling, letting Landon in. And as good as it feels right now, it's dangerous. When you care, you open yourself up to pain. Most of the time, I think it's better to keep your distance. It might be lonely, but at least it's safe.

Landon parks next to my Jeep and turns off the key. He stares out the front window and drums his fingers over the wheel a few times before he turns to me. Like him, I'm still in my seat, not wanting to leave...but not sure I should stay.

He doesn't say anything. He just sits there, studying me with his eyebrows slightly drawn together and his lips pressed into a thin line. And, *oh,* those lips.

I need to say something, diffuse the situation. The air feels so charged, I'm surprised it's not sizzling.

Looking away, I unclip my seatbelt. "Well, I think that went all right, all things considered."

"It did," he agrees.

I give him a big, flirty smile. "And I suppose we've concluded we don't necessarily need to practice...our...um..."

A smirk plays at the corner of Landon's mouth as I flounder to finish the sentence.

"Chemistry?" he offers, his expression perfectly serious except for a hint of a devilish smile.

"Yeah. That."

Unable to stand the tension any longer, I open my door and step into the night. Landon does the same, and just as I'm softly shutting the door, he rounds the front and steps into my space. "But it might have been a fluke," he says in an impartial voice that makes it seem as if our daydream-inducing kiss was nothing more than a science experiment.

I impulsively step back. "What?"

He cocks his head to the side. "The chemistry."

My mouth goes dry.

"We should probably test it again—just to be sure." He takes another step in.

I find myself nodding. *Yes, test it. Of course we must.*

He shifts like he's going to pull me into his arms. "We'll have to try it again soon, just to be sure." His voice is a velvet caress, and I feel myself slipping.

Just when I think *soon* might mean *now*, he steps back. "Night, Lacey."

I blink several times and then stand a bit straighter. "Right...night. You too."

He follows me as I turn to walk to the back porch. I set my hand on the doorknob, reluctant to leave just yet. Landon waits until I open the door before he jogs down the steps. "See you tomorrow. Maybe we can grab a pizza? I still haven't tried the place in town."

"Okay," I say, feeling a bit dazed.

Standing halfway inside the door, I watch him drive around the front of the house and don't go inside until the crunch of the gravel fades.

"How was your date?" Mom asks when I step into the

living room. She and Uncle Mark are on the couch, watching a movie.

Not a date. We might have held hands, kissed, and ended the night with him walking me to the door...but *it wasn't a date.*

Mark pauses the movie so I can answer. He and Mom turn their eyes on me, both too attentive. I know they're trying to show interest in my life, but it's awkward.

"It was fine." I sit on the arm of the chair next to the couch.

"You're home early."

"The party got a little wild, and Misty shut it down."

Mom narrows her eyes. "How wild?"

"I didn't drink or do drugs if that's what you're asking."

Appeased, she nods.

"Good job, kiddo," Uncle Mark says and then offers to restart the movie so we all can watch.

I decline and start for my bedroom, but before I'm out the door, Mom says, "You're okay, right? You had fun with Landon?"

My heart twinges because I'm more than okay, and I had a little too much fun.

I like Landon. Like, really like him.

Which is probably bad.

CHAPTER FOURTEEN

A KNOCK at the door pulls me from my laptop. Earlier today, the Tillmans posted the video that contained the footage of Landon and me at the bonfire. It already has thousands of views.

The comments are enough to make my head spin. Dozens of people ask if Landon and I are together. Some people gush about how cute we are; others seem upset Landon's already moved on to another girl.

Why do they care? Honestly, some people are just obsessive. (Thinks the girl who's watched the video half a dozen times already.)

Leaving my laptop on the couch, I answer the door, fully expecting Paige.

Busy with Tanner, she hasn't been around as much lately. She'll get bored and break it off eventually, and then I'll see more of her again.

Ours is a stable friendship, and I don't mind. Especially since she sends me emoji-filled texts several times a day just so I don't feel ignored.

Still, Tanner's lasted longer than I expected, and I don't like it. I have this awful feeling about him, and I'll be glad when he's out of the picture.

But it's not Paige on the other side of the door.

"Hi," I say, startled to find Landon.

We haven't talked since the party. In fact, I didn't see him all weekend. I'm sure it has nothing to do with the fact that I've been hiding in the house.

"You're avoiding me again." He crosses his arms and leans against the door frame. His light green eyes are bright despite his serious tone.

Just seeing him does funny things to my stomach.

"No," I protest, stepping aside so he can come in. "I've been...busy."

"Oh yeah?" He nods toward the open laptop, displaying the paused video, and a grin steals across his face. "What's that you're working on?"

I rush over to the computer and snap it shut. "Not that."

He raises his eyebrows, waiting.

Giving in, I plop onto the couch, motioning for him to join me. "Gray Jay celebrates its anniversary in the middle of July, and the campground hosts a barbecue every year. I decided to make flyers this year, but I'm not very good at it."

Self-conscious, I open the laptop and quickly close the browser, revealing the sad design. Even I can tell it looks terrible.

"You even work while you're at home," he jokes.

I roll my eyes as Landon pulls the laptop onto his lap.

"This is..." he begins, trying to hide a grimace.

"Awful."

He laughs. "I was going to say a good start."

He's so close, his leg presses against mine. I try not to think about it—and definitely try not to think about our kiss, though that's an impossible mission.

"Care if I tweak things?" he asks, gesturing to the screen.

"Be my guest. In fact, start over."

Anything he comes up with has to be better than what I had.

Immediately engrossed in his task, Landon opens a new screen, uploads a few pictures from his phone, and gets to work. After a few minutes, unable to handle sitting so close to him, I wander into the kitchen, leaving him to it.

"What are you doing in there?" he calls after a while.

I put the finishing touches on two chocolate chip cookie sundaes and bring them into the living room. I sit next to him...though not as close as before.

"You are the best faux girlfriend I've ever had," he says, greedily accepting the ice cream.

"Have you had many?"

He smirks and takes a massive, boy-sized bite. It should be disgusting, but it only makes me laugh. As he eats, he continues to work.

I watch him, more than a little impressed. As I finish

the last bit of caramel syrup at the bottom of my dish, I tell him, "You're really good at this."

"I hope so." He makes a few final tweaks. "I'm thinking about studying graphic design."

"You definitely should."

The finished flyer looks incredibly professional—in fact, it looks like we hired someone to make it. And it took him less than thirty minutes.

"Thank you," I say, wholeheartedly meaning it.

He saves the file and closes the computer. "Don't think too highly of me. My motives were entirely selfish."

Our eyes meet, and I'm unable to look away. "How is that?"

"I'm bored, and you've locked yourself away for the last few days. Now you have no excuse to avoid me."

"I wasn't avoid—"

"Yeah, okay," he says with a laugh. His phone rings as he's dragging me off the couch.

He pulls it from his pocket, and the smile drops from his face. The phone continues to ring, and he stares at the number.

"Landon?" I ask, growing a bit worried.

He looks up. "It's Evie."

"Evie...like, your Evie?" And though it's none of my business, I feel sick.

He's already shoving the cell back into his pocket, but I put on a nonchalant expression. "You can answer it if you want."

"Should I?" he asks, unsure.

No, I think, but I say, "Why not?"

He nods, hesitant, and then answers the call. But not like I expect.

"Why are you calling, Evie?" he asks, his tone flat.

It would be enough to send chills down my spine if I were on the other line.

"We're not together anymore," he responds to her answer, and this time his tone is a little softer. "And it really isn't your concern."

She must have seen the video, which means she's still watching the channel. If I were to take a guess, I'd say she still has feelings for Landon.

I turn away, worried I'm intruding, but there's nowhere for me to go. It would be rude to leave Landon alone in my living room, wouldn't it? Well, that's the excuse I'm going to use so I don't feel so guilty about eavesdropping.

"It's Lacey, not Stacey," he corrects, making me wonder if she messed my name up on purpose. Unable to help myself, I turn back to face him. Our eyes meet, and he holds my gaze. Then, enunciating each word with precision, he says, "I like her. A lot."

Tingles travel my spine, spreading to my limbs. The way Landon's looking at me, the way he's holding my eyes, makes me think that he means it. That maybe he said it for my benefit, not in response to something his ex-girlfriend said.

He ends the call a few moments later, and I look away, feeling a bit overwhelmed. What's happening here? This pretend relationship is starting to feel like more.

"I'm hungry," he says out of the blue, sliding the phone back into his pocket.

I look back. "What?"

He offers his hand. "Let's get hamburgers."

I stare at his palm. "We just had huge sundaes. How are you hungry?"

"I'm a guy—it's kind of our thing." He wiggles his fingers, waiting for me to accept the invitation.

Giving in, I take his hand. There's something sweet about holding hands, something indescribably fulfilling.

It's also extremely intimate, in some ways more so than kissing. And it scares me.

But it's exhilarating too. As Landon leads me from the house, I decide to focus on that and push my doubts aside.

We walk out the door and find Mom and Uncle Mark in the front. She's leaning into him, and he has his arms wrapped around her back.

"What's wrong?" I ask, instantly concerned.

"Nothing." She steps away, and Mark's arms fall to his sides. "Just a typical Monday. Hi, Landon."

"Hey, Mrs. Morrison."

"Cassie is fine," she says, cracking a smile.

"What happened?" I prod, not about to let her avoid the question.

She rolls her shoulders. "I mixed up spaces and sent a couple to an occupied site. Instead of letting me know, they chose their own. Thirty minutes later, I sent another couple to *that* spot, and it created all kinds of chaos."

"We fixed it," Mark adds.

I frown. "Did you use my laminated campground chart? Maybe I forgot to mark off the spot. I should probably go through it and double check it for current occupancy." I'm already tugging away from Landon, heading toward the office.

"I just forgot to look at it," she says, brushing it off. Then she changes the subject. "Where are you two headed?"

"We're going out for hamburgers," Landon says.

I glance in the direction of the office. "I should probably take a quick look—"

Mom laughs in a frustrated way. "Lacey, it's fine."

Biting the inside of my cheek, I finally nod.

"*Go,*" she says, making shooing motions with her hands.

Giving in—but not necessarily happy about it—I let Landon lead me away.

We make the unspoken agreement to walk. It's a good trek to Main Street, but it's a beautiful day with a cool breeze, and we have sundaes to work off before I'll be able to eat again.

Landon still has my hand, and we walk side by side, in no rush.

"I have a weird question, but I don't know how you'll take it," he says after several minutes.

I give him a questioning look.

"Would you be upset if your mom and uncle ever got together?"

"They're *not* together."

He gently tugs me back when I try to yank away. "But would it bother you if they were?"

My mom wouldn't do that to my dad, and neither would Uncle Mark. Doesn't anyone get that? It would be a betrayal to his memory. Who makes a move on their dead brother's widow? Just...ew.

"They're really good friends," I explain again. "And Mark *is* like a dad to me, but I swear their relationship isn't like that."

"Okay."

That's all he says. Just "okay." Which is a little obnoxious because I know it means he doesn't agree, but he doesn't want to argue.

"It's *not*."

Landon laughs, shaking his head. "I believe you, Lacey. I was just asking."

And I let it go because I like the way he says my name, like we're close. Like I'm his, and he's mine, and we're actually together.

"Where has the best burgers?" he asks, putting the previous conversation behind us.

But even though we've changed the subject, my mind stays on his question. I remember the way Mom was leaning into Mark for comfort, and I'm plagued with niggling doubts.

But she wouldn't do that to Dad. I know it.

———

A GLOP OF STICKY, white paint runs down the split

rail fence that separates the campground from the road. I mop up my mess with a big, fat brush I found in the back shed.

Yesterday, I noticed the fence was looking a little shabby. Since it's the first thing people see when they pull up, I decided it needed a fresh coat. Mark said the project has been on his to-do list for months, but he hasn't gotten around to it yet.

"You realize it's the Fourth of July?" Paige calls as she walks up the road from the direction of her family's property. A gust of wind tosses her long hair in front of her eyes and kicks up leaves and dirt.

Unfortunately, those leaves stick to my fence.

"Yeah," I mutter, plucking bits of debris out of the wet paint.

"They canceled the fireworks due to the wind," my friend informs me as she stops in front of the fence and admires my work. "You missed a spot."

Normally, I would tell her to grab a brush, but I haven't seen her in days, and I'm reluctant to put her to work. "I thought they might," I say, referring to the fireworks. Then I realize she's alone. "Where's Tanner?"

She bites back a besotted grin and stares at the fence with a dreamy expression that worries me. "His family drove to Telluride for the weekend. They're supposed to be back Monday."

"Whatever are you going to do with all your free time?"

"I'm going to fetch a paintbrush because it's obvious you're rubbish at this."

I roll my eyes, but I'm glad for the help, so I don't argue. What started as a simple project has grown. The fence seems to be getting longer. At this rate, I'm not sure I'll ever finish.

"Take a break," Paige says. "Help me find a brush."

Gladly, I set my own brush aside and stretch my back as I rise.

"Where's your fake boyfriend?" she asks as we make our way to the shed.

"He's helping his dad with video stuff. They're having trouble with one of the computers."

Instead of answering, Paige nods to a patch of dirt near the gazebo. "Isn't that a little Tillman? What's he doing?"

"He's looking for gold."

Paige flashes me an incredulous look.

"No, I'm serious. Caleb's been completely obsessed since he found a book about it at our house when they first arrived. Somehow, he figured out that our gravel came from a local quarry, and he asked Uncle Mark if he could search through it to see if he can find something valuable. He's been at it for *days*."

"Okay then..." Paige says, just as baffled as I am.

"Hi, Hunter," I call to Landon's second youngest brother. The boy sits in the gazebo, poking at his phone, looking bored as can be. He must be on Caleb duty this afternoon. Watching the spirited eight-year-old is a full-time job, and everyone in the family takes turns.

Hunter looks up and raises a listless hand in greeting before he goes back to his screen.

"Find anything?" I ask Caleb.

His head is bent over in extreme concentration, and he doesn't stop sorting long enough to even look up. "Not yet."

"Well, good luck," I call as we walk past.

Still staring at the ground, he says, "Yep."

"I saw the Tillman's latest video," Paige says as we enter the shed.

"Oh yeah?" I can't quite bring myself to look at her, so I search for an extra brush instead.

"You two look awfully couple-ish."

"That's kind of the point."

"I thought maybe you had forgotten that point and dropped the *fake* in fake dating."

I remember how Landon told Evie he likes me, and my cheeks heat. Hopefully, Paige can't tell in the dim light.

"Nope."

"If you say so." She spots a brush poking out from under a folded blue tarp and pulls it off the shelf. "This should work."

The rest of the afternoon passes quickly, and we somehow manage to finish the fence before dinner.

As we're cleaning up, Paige's phone rings. "Hey," she coos as soon as she answers.

I wrinkle my nose.

"*Tanner*," she giggles, making me ill.

Resisting the strong urge to gag, I finish cleaning the brushes as she talks, and then I rinse out the pan with a garden hose. Across the way, Mom and Uncle Mark catch my eye.

Her hand is on his arm, and they're awfully close. I freeze, feeling uneasy, but they split a moment later. Mark goes one way, and Mom heads the other.

I shake my head, determined to believe I'm reading too much into things.

CHAPTER FIFTEEN

THE OSCILLATING FAN on the counter does little to cool the hot office. After months of cold, fickle spring weather, summer decides to hit with a vengeance.

The bells above the front door chime, and in walk Greg and Hallie.

"How's the fishing?" I ask Greg.

"It's great—thanks again for the cabin on the water."

"No problem." I set aside the newly printed stack of flyers advertising Saturday's barbecue. Soon, I need to distribute them throughout the campground. If I have time, I might even go into town and hang them in shop windows. "What can I do for you guys?"

Hallie stands next to Greg, reading the kids' craft schedule. "You're panning for gold Saturday?" she asks.

Surprised she's talking, I turn to her. "Sort of. We're going to spray rocks with gold paint and hide them in a kiddie pool of sand. The kids will get to 'pan' for them, and then they can trade in their gold for little prizes or candy—kind of like the ticket system at arcades."

I found the idea online and was inspired by Caleb, who's so obsessed with finding gold. Much to his chagrin, he hasn't found anything valuable in our landscaping. (He did, however, catch a lizard that entertained him for half a day.)

"That's fun," she says. "You put a lot of thought into your activities."

It's why we charge "the big bucks," as Uncle Mark jokes, but I don't tell Hallie that. Everyone who stays here knows you get what you pay for.

"Thanks. I think they'll have a good time with it."

"We're here for the pool code," Greg says.

"It's open from seven to ten," I tell them as I write down the five-digit number, glancing up when the door opens. Landon walks in but hangs back. He wears a small smile as he waits for me to finish with the Hendricks.

I hand Hallie the number. "If you're going in the next few hours, I'd be happy to watch Bark for you—I remember you saying he doesn't like to be alone. Mom's coming in for office duty shortly, and I was going to walk the campground and hand out flyers."

"Really?" Hallie asks.

"Sure. He's welcome to come with me."

"You guys really are awesome," Hallie says with a laugh. I think she might finally be opening up. "I'll bring him by in fifteen minutes. If it's really all right."

"Of course."

Landon waits until they're out the door before he

ambles over, looking entirely too tempting in shorts and a T-shirt that's just fitted enough to show a hint of muscle —a scrumptious hint.

"Hi, Faux Boyfriend," I say, teasing him...and reminding myself at the same time.

"Hi to you too, Faux—" He cuts off abruptly as Mom walks into the office.

She calls a greeting back to the Hendricks as she enters.

"Hey, Landon," she says, a big smile stretching across her face. Her hair is still down for the day—surprising considering how hot it is. "What are you guys up to this afternoon?"

I hold up my new stack of flyers. "The Hendricks are going to bring Bark by, and we're going to walk around the sites to hand these out."

"But I said you could have the afternoon off." Mom frowns in the way that makes me feel bad for being *too* productive—which is weird.

"It's just walking—not exactly hard work," I point out.

Mom takes a flyer, and her eyebrows jump with surprise. "These are awesome. Did you make them?"

"Landon designed them," I say, flashing him a smirk. "I ate ice cream."

Mom turns toward Landon and beams. "At least you can get her to take time off."

"I do my best," he says.

Does he ever.

She digs into her pocket and tries to hand several twenties to Landon. "Thank you for the design."

He steps back, refusing to take the money. "It was nothing."

"Use it to take my daughter out. Drive into the city and catch a movie or something."

Watching with wry amusement, I cross my arms. "Are you actually paying a guy to take me on a date? Thanks, Mom."

She grins and waves the bills at Landon, not about to back down. Apparently coming to the correct conclusion that she's more stubborn than he is, Landon gives in and accepts the money, solemnly promising it will be spent on me very soon.

Hallie shows up with Bark just as Landon pockets the bills. The Greyhound trots on his lead, right by Hallie's side, and plops his rump down the moment she stops.

"Are you sure he won't be any trouble?" Hallie asks, dressed in a swimsuit and flip-flops, with a beach towel wrapped around her middle. "He can be rambunctious."

Bark stares at me, the picture of manners.

"Positive," I assure her.

She thanks me again—many times. Before she leaves, she turns back. "Oh, watch out. He likes squirrels."

Thinking she's joking, I laugh.

Hallie widens her eyes and shakes her head. "No. He *really* likes squirrels."

"I'll be careful," I swear.

Before she leaves, she kneels in front of Bark and tells him to be good. The dog wags his skinny tail.

"Good boy," she kisses his head, apparently as attached to him as McKenna is Candy, and finally walks out the door.

"Whatever you do, don't lose that dog," Mom jokes as she sits at the desk, ready to do her time. I almost remind her to check my laminated chart before she assigns any sites, but I hold my tongue.

"We'll be fine." I look down. "Won't we, Bark?"

He watches me with his adoring, liquid brown eyes.

"See?"

Landon offers to take the flyers, and he follows me out the door. Bark trots with us, perfect as can be.

"That dog is putting Candy and George to shame," Landon jokes.

"He is really good, isn't he?" I ask, and then I give Landon a nudge. "So, are you going to keep me company while I hand these out?"

Landon slides his arm through mine, tugging me close to his side. "We have appearances to keep up, don't we?"

I tell myself that's the candy-coated part of the already sweet deal. I get all the perks of dating Landon without any of the heartbreak. I just have to deny my heart is getting tangled up to believe it.

"I see you have your camera," I say when he pulls the device from his pocket and begins recording. I've seen his parents with a bigger one, one with a fluffy audio accessory and larger lenses. Landon seems partial to simplicity.

He focuses it on me. "Never leave home without it."

I'm growing used to its constant presence.

"Tell me, Lacey, what are we doing today?" he asks in an exaggerated voice.

"Well, *Landon*, we're going to hand out flyers for the barbecue."

"And who is walking with us?"

I smile, loving the lighthearted way he handles his videos. Sometimes he's a bit over-the-top—but in a completely endearing way. No wonder the family has so many subscribers. "This is Bark."

He films as we walk, switching to a natural, conversation mode for his viewers. We make our way through the campground, handing out flyers and chatting with people. The retirees like to talk in particular—especially to the camera.

Some of them have been coming to the campground every summer for as long as I can remember. They dole out hugs when they first see me and tell me how "grown-up" I look. Then they focus on Landon's camera, detailing every stop they've made from the moment they pulled out of our campground at the end of last summer to the day they returned. Not only does Landon not mind, but he nods as they talk, giving them his full attention.

I'm standing here, most of the flyers distributed, listening to Mr. Pent tell us about the alligator they found underneath their Class A motorhome while they were snow-birding in Florida, when Bark spots a squirrel.

"No!" I yell as Bark pulls a canine version of Dr.

Jekyll to Mr. Hyde and rips from my grasp, running down the camp road, chasing after the bushy-tailed rodent that's barely evading him. "Bark!"

I take off after him, flyers flying behind me, desperate to catch Hallie Hendrick's beloved dog. Even at his age, he's crazy fast.

Landon's right behind me, and then he passes me completely, far quicker than I am since I'm in flip-flops. We race through the campground, through A Loop, through the thick brush to B Loop, and then the squirrel finally darts up a pine tree and disappears.

Bark stops under the tree, leaping three feet into the air, trying to find a way up.

I slow to a walk as soon as Landon grabs the dog's leash and set my hands on my hips, gulping precious air. Apparently, I need to get more exercise.

"Thank you," I say to Landon as I attempt to catch my breath.

Like an angel, Bark forgets about the squirrel, plops onto his haunches, and wags his tail, practically saying, "Aren't I a good boy?"

"You're rotten," I inform him.

His tongue lolls out, and his tail wags faster.

"You're all scratched up," Landon informs me, nodding to my legs.

I glance down and find several minor white scratches along with a long one that's oozing blood. "Oh, yuck. I must have caught myself in the bushes."

"Come on." Landon's already walking toward the

office. "Let's drop off the mighty squirrel hunter with your mom, and I'll fix you up."

Ten minutes later, we're in Landon's camper, and he's digging through the overhead cupboards while I try not to bleed on his mother's cushions.

"Where's your family?" I ask, eyeing the white cat as she comes out of her hiding place so she can study me from the table. When I attempt to pet her, she steps just far enough away I can't reach her and continues to stare.

"They took the dogs on a hike." Landon comes to the cupboard directly above me and rummages through it.

"And why aren't you hiking?" I ask, looking down so I'm not staring at his stomach.

Finding what he's looking for, he kneels in front of me, first aid kit in his hand. "Because I'm with you."

Butterflies flutter, but I ignore them. It's just a side effect of being around Landon.

"You ready for this?" he asks as he opens an anti-septic wipe. "I don't know what brand these are, but they sting like no other."

Before I have a chance to answer, Landon dabs the wipe along the long, deep cut. I suck in a hiss, laughing at the same time.

"Told you." His gaze meets mine, and even though he's not smiling, his eyes are.

"You have pretty eyes," I say out of nowhere. Instantly, I wish I could take it back.

Because I'm watching him so closely, I see the way those aforementioned eyes widen with surprise and then scrunch with amusement. "Pretty, huh?"

I feel the all-familiar blush heating my cheeks. "You know what I mean."

"When did you get this?" He runs the pad of his thumb over an inch-long scar on the inside of my knee.

"Riding my bike when I was about nine," I answer, pretending it doesn't faze me that his hand is on my leg. "I caught it on a jagged rock."

Landon meets my gaze again. "Sounds more like crashing than riding."

"Yeah."

All I can think about is our kiss...kisses...that night in Misty's barn. The thought completely consumes me. From the way Landon's eyes darken, I wonder if he's thinking of the same thing. Just the memory makes me nibble my bottom lip. When his eyes follow the movement, I panic.

"I don't think we should kiss again," I blurt out.

Very slowly, looking far too amused, he raises his eyebrows. "All right."

"Not that you were going to... I mean, I'm not trying to say you were thinking about..."

Shut up already, Lacey. Just. Shut. Up.

"I was," he says, his eyes still locked on mine.

"Oh."

Oh.

"But if you think it's a bad idea, we won't." His thumb moves tiny circles over the sensitive spot on my inner knee.

"I don't date summer boys," I explain at a whisper. "Not anymore. Not actually."

Landon nods, but there's something in his expression that causes my stomach to tighten in the most delightful way. "Sounds reasonable."

Does it?

"We should probably..." I motion to the first aid kit.

A smirk tugs at his lips, and I'm having trouble reading him. With careful hands, he applies ointment to the pads of several regular-sized bandages and places them in a row over the long scratch, one by one. I watch him in silence, mesmerized.

When he's finished, he zips up the first-aid kit and offers me a hand. "Don't worry, we'll keep it platonic," he promises.

"Okay." I nod like that's a good thing—a wise thing.

I'm an idiot.

Just as I'm walking toward the door, silently scolding myself for the rash words, Landon catches me around the waist and pulls me back. "Except in public, right?"

My pulse jumps, and I try not to melt against him. "Naturally."

We have appearances to keep up after all...

His eyes practically sparkle. "Then it's settled. I'll only kiss you in public."

And though that statement is all wrong, I nod like it makes perfect sense.

"Okay," I say, breathless.

Grinning, Landon releases me and heads down the camper stairs, into the sunshine...hopefully toward a public place.

CHAPTER SIXTEEN

A MAN WALKS into the office wearing pressed khakis, a butter-colored polo shirt, and tan loafers. My first instinct is to ask him if he's lost.

"Can I help you?" I ask.

He spots my mother's sculpture near the front counter. "As a matter of fact, I believe you can. I'm looking for Cassie Morrison."

For one terrifying moment, I wonder if this man is from the bank. But then I remember the campground's paid and clear, and I'm left with no clue who he might be or why he's asking for my mother.

"She's not in right now. Do you want me to give her a call?"

"Would you mind?"

I'm about to ask him for his info when he beats me to it by flipping a sharp and glossy business card on the counter between us.

"All right, Mr. ..." I peer at the card. "Albert. Let me

see if I can reach her. Cell service is a little spotty around here."

He gives me an amused, closed-mouth smile. "I've noticed."

Instead of calling, I text. *There's a fussy-looking man here asking about you. Do you want me to tell him you're in your studio?*

I set the phone aside, smiling pleasantly. I'm not entirely sure she'll answer—after all, I wasn't lying when I said the cell service stinks.

But a few moments later, my phone chimes. *Who is he?*

I glance at the card and type, *Fredrick Albert, Head Curator at the Denver—*

Whoa. Hold up.

Who is this guy?

"I buy art," the man says, his eyes scrunched in the corners. He's obviously amused by my reaction. "I saw Cassie's work on a YouTube video."

"Right," I say, giving him a curious smile, growing excited. Mrs. Tillman gushed about a few of Mom's pieces a few weeks ago. Somehow, this man must have found the video.

I finish the text, and two seconds later, Mom responds, *Send him over.*

"She's in her studio," I tell him, setting the phone aside. It's the first cabin after you pass the house—the little one in the trees."

Send Mark over just in case he's a serial killer, Mom texts as an afterthought.

I glance at Mr. Albert, worried he might have seen what she wrote, but he's already headed for the door.

After I send Uncle Mark a text, I try to focus on my work, a task that's not so easy when Landon comes walking in the door.

"You busy?" he asks.

"Nope." I bite back a grin. "I just like to sit in front of the computer and work on spreadsheets for the fun of it."

He chuckles and rests his tall self against the counter. "With anyone else, that might be sarcasm, but with you, I'm not sure."

"Do you need something?"

"You," he says lightly, but the words make me flush.

"Oh yeah?"

"I have been instructed to invite my *girlfriend* over for dinner. Dad's smoking ribs, and Mom and McKenna are putting the finishing touches on a three-layer Black Forest cake."

"Both of those are impressive feats to undertake in a camper," I say lightly, trying to hide the fact that hearing him call me his girlfriend does funny things to my pulse. "Black Forest...that means chocolate, right?"

"Indeed." He leans down lower, meeting my eyes. "So what do you say? Want to brave my family for the evening?"

I give him a one-shouldered shrug. "Maybe. Because there's cake."

His answering grin is fast, and it does nothing to settle my humming nerves. "I'll meet you when you're finished, and we'll walk together."

"Okay." I realize I've typed the same number twice. "Now go away. You're distracting me."

"Oh, yeah?" He raises his eyebrows, openly flirting. "Like a good distraction?"

"*Go.*"

———

DONE FOR THE DAY, I lock the office. As Landon walks with me to his site, he tells me how Hunter dropped their dad's expensive camera this afternoon. It seems to be in working order, but Hunter's still pouting, so I've been warned that he might not be in the best mood.

Though, with Hunter, how can you tell the difference between a good mood and a bad one?

"You okay?" Landon asks when we're close to the campsite.

I've been around the Tillmans dozens of times now, but for some reason, I'm incredibly nervous this evening.

I almost jump at the question. "Hmm? Oh, I'm just preparing myself. I'm still new at this fake girlfriend stuff."

He gives me a funny look, like he wants to say something but changes his mind.

"I'm a little nervous," I admit.

"It will be fine," he answers, looking ahead. "Just pretend it's real."

Because *that* will help.

Then, for the sake of the ruse, Landon takes my hand. I swallow back a surprised giggle.

McKenna runs toward us as soon as she spots us walking up the road. Tethered to her leash, which is attached to the picnic table, Candy yelps, trying to follow. To her dismay, she realizes she can go no farther than the trailer door.

George lifts his head to see what the racket is all about. He wags his tail a few times when he sees us and then yawns and goes back to napping.

The most delicious-smelling campfire smoke wafts our way, making my stomach growl. Judging from the spicy, sweet aroma, Mr. Tillman's ribs are going to be amazing. All the nearby campers must be jealous.

"Hey, Lacey." Landon's dad raises a pair of tongs in greeting. "Glad to have you."

"Thanks," I say, though I'm hit with another bout of nerves.

Landon lightly touches my shoulder after he lets go of my hand. "Want something to drink?"

I nod.

"Did you throw extra drinks in the cooler?" he asks his Dad.

"Yeah, there's all kinds of stuff in there. I think William and Barbara are going to stop by in a bit, so I wanted to make sure we had plenty."

Landon digs through the ice in the cooler and pulls several options to the top.

"William and Barbara from Site Fifteen?" I choose a

bottle of lemon-lime soda, hoping sipping it will ease my nerves.

Mr. Tillman opens the tabletop smoker, letting out a billowing cloud of barbecue-scented heaven. "That's right. Barbara has been helping Sarah piece together the quilt she's been working on down at the community center."

So that's where Mrs. Tillman has been sewing that quilt. I wondered how she managed it in the RV. Gray Jay's community center is tiny—just a restored Victorian house on Main Street, but it's a favorite hangout for crafty ladies much older than Landon's mother.

"Hi there, Lacey," Landon's mom says, walking through the camper door with a massive bowl of potato salad in one hand and a tossed salad in the other.

Caleb comes running out behind his mother. "I got a geode!" he tells me.

"You did? From where?"

"The rock and mineral shop in town, like you suggested the other day," Hunter says, coming down the steps behind his brother, looking about as chipper as always.

Caleb scowls at him. "It's my story."

Hunter rolls his eyes, sits at the picnic table, and pulls out his phone.

"Landon broke it open earlier," Caleb continues, turning back to me. "Do you want to see it?"

I nod, and he scurries back into the camper, off to retrieve his treasure.

"Is he over his gold fascination?" I ask Landon quietly.

He shakes his head. "No. He talked to the man at the shop for thirty minutes about the history of mining in the area."

Colorado is perhaps known more for its silver and uranium than gold, but we had a short rush of our own in the eighteen hundreds.

"Are the ribs done?" Mrs. Tillman asks her husband as she places the bowls in the middle of the picnic table. She's already set it with a brightly striped tablecloth and lit several jar candles. In the middle of the table, there's a bowl of hot pink flowers, something she must have planted since they're going to be here all summer.

The Tillmans are better at this camping thing than most.

"Yep, we're ready to eat," Landon's dad confirms.

You don't have to tell the younger boys twice. Caleb and Hunter leap in, though Landon holds back with me. After we fill our plates, we sit in camp chairs scattered around the site. It's all very casual, and it sets me at ease—even if Landon is right next to me.

But no matter how many times I tell myself this isn't real, I catch myself feeling like maybe it is. That's crazy though. I'd know if something had shifted between us...

Wouldn't I?

"Can I bring out the cake?" McKenna asks her mom after the last of the leftovers have been spirited away.

"Yes, but be careful," Mrs. Tillman instructs.

Nodding solemnly, McKenna walks into the camper.

Several moments later, she appears at the door with a gorgeous cake precariously teetering in her hands. She pauses at the top of the stairs, frowning in concentration.

"Don't trip," Mr. Tillman says.

She's just coming down the last step when Candy spots a dog walking with his owners on the road. The little cotton puff runs in front of McKenna, tripping the girl with her sparkly pink leash. McKenna tumbles forward, shrieking.

Landon leaps up, grabbing McKenna before she can fall face first on the ground, and he ends up with a shirt-full of chocolate cherry cake. Everyone is silent for several moments, and then Caleb glares at Candy and loudly proclaims, "Stupid mutt!"

"*Caleb*," Mrs. Tillman reprimands, standing to relieve McKenna of the empty plate. McKenna's lower jaw trembles as she surveys the mess.

"Don't cry," her mom says, though she looks as heart-broken about the loss of perfectly good chocolate as the next person. "It was just an accident. No one's mad at you."

Hunter watches silently, looking conflicted. It's obvious he's amused that his older brother got caked...but at the same time, he's irked that now there's no cake. It's quite a predicament. I'm not sure which emotion is winning.

Mrs. Tillman turns to Landon and frowns. "We'll take your shirt to the laundry room when it opens in the morning."

I eye the fudge chocolate and thick cherry pie filling

as it goops down the front of Landon's stomach.

"You can use our washer," I volunteer.

Landon turns to me, and I get a full view of the mess. A jagged piece of cake falls to his feet, followed by a gob of frosting. I try not to laugh...but I fail.

He cracks a smile, and soon we're all laughing to the point that our stomachs hurt, and we can't breathe.

"Come on," I tell Landon once I catch my breath, motioning for him to follow me.

We say goodbye to the rest of the Tillmans and head to my house. It's such a nice evening; most campers are out and about. They sit around campfires, waiting for dark. We get some pretty weird looks when they spot Landon. He acknowledges them with friendly greetings, but we don't stop until we reach my house.

The front door is locked, so we go around the back. It's locked too.

"Mom must have gone out," I explain, and then I pull a key out of my back pocket. Even though it's just dusky outside, it's dark inside, so I flip on the lights in the kitchen as we enter.

As soon as my phone connects to the internet, a text message comes through, assisted by our WiFi. I read it and then toss my phone on the counter. "Mom and Mark went for dinner in town, and then they're going to drive down to the city to watch a movie."

"What's the chance I'm going to get this all in my hair?" Landon asks.

I turn to face him, and then I freeze. His shirt is

halfway over his head, and I'm left with an eyeful of toned stomach and chest.

"The chances are pretty good," I say absently.

He pulls off the shirt, turning it inside out so it doesn't make a horrific mess.

"Well?" he asks, flashing me a knee-weakening grin.

My mouth goes dry. "Well...what?"

His eyes glint with humor. "Am I covered in chocolate?"

Unbidden, my feet shuffle forward until I'm right in front of him. There's chocolate on his collarbone, neck, a little on his jaw, and just a bit in his hair.

"Yeah," I say. My voice sounds off, even to my own ears.

His smile flickers with something even more delicious than the icing. He rubs his neck, trying to get the frosting off. "Where?"

Never in my life have I shown this much restraint. I should win an award.

"Um," I hover my hand over him, pointing out spots. "Here, here, here, and here... Just a minute. I'll get you a paper towel."

I turn from him, needing to put space between us, and walk to the sink. Is it sweltering in here? We should open a few more windows...

I wet a handful of paper towels and turn...only to find him right in front of me.

"Here you go," I say brightly, trying to keep my eyes on his face and off his chest. It's a very nice chest...the kind athletes have. A soccer player's chest.

Landon takes the paper towels, but his eyes are on mine. The air gets a little too thick to breathe. "Thanks," he says.

"Yep."

I rest my lower back against the counter as he dabs at his neck, watching as he misses the chocolate completely. I could lead him to a mirror...or I could do it myself. That's allowed, right? I mean, I'm just helping.

People aren't helpful enough anymore—Mom used to tell me that all the time when I was younger.

I hold out my hand. "Want me to..."

He steps a smidgen closer. "Sure."

I carefully dab at his skin, wiping the frosting away. We're close and getting closer.

"So," I say, desperately needing to keep my mouth busy talking so I don't do something reckless. "Did you play sports when you were younger?"

"Lacrosse," he says.

"Oh." I wipe frosting off his jaw. "We don't have that at our school. I think I've seen it on television though. It's like a ball game with butterfly nets, right?"

He steps in, close enough I can feel the heat coming off his skin. Oh, this is bad. What are we doing? This isn't how people who are pretending to be in a relationship act when they're alone.

"Something like that." There's amusement in his voice, but he's lowered it, dropped it to a silky almost-whisper.

"We're not in public," I remind him when he brushes

his lips against my jaw. It's my last noble effort to keep things simple.

"No, we're not."

"I thought we weren't going to—"

"I changed my mind."

"Okay?" Oddly it comes out like a question.

"Okay?" he chuckles under his breath. "What does that—"

"*Kiss me already.*"

His eyes lock with mine, and time stands still. Then, waking from the trance, Landon's hands fly to the sides of my waist, and he pulls me to him. Our mouths meet in a kiss that neither of us can pretend has anything to do with us practicing our chemistry or furthering the cause of our ruse. I let my hands drift to his chest...which is a bad idea considering he's still rather shirtless.

You have five more seconds, that little voice says, though even it's losing intensity. Landon doesn't hesitate this time, and to my surprise, neither do I. I pour myself into the kiss—hold nothing back, and he meets me.

I lean against the counter, accidentally knocking a cup into the sink, making a dreadful racket. We abruptly break apart and blink at each other, both of us out of breath and slightly dazed. Suddenly, I realize how quiet it is. The grandfather clock in the living room ticks with each passing second, and the sound becomes deafening.

Landon's eyes search mine, and his fingers tighten on my sides. I gulp. We've crossed a line—a very serious line. And I want to do it again. In fact, I want to erase the line, scratch it out, wash it away and pretend we never created it.

His chest moves with each labored breath, betraying the fact that he's as shaken as I am. "Are we—"

Before he can finish, I stand on my toes and wrap my hand around the back of his neck, dragging his lips down to mine. He chuckles darkly, a sound that makes my knees wobble, and meets me with fervor.

And then the front door opens.

"Lacey," Mom calls. "Are you home? We're back."

CHAPTER SEVENTEEN

WE RIP APART, eyes wide, staring at each other for several incredulous seconds before Landon leaps back and jumps for the sink. He's innocently washing out his shirt when Mom and Mark walk into the kitchen.

Mom's eyebrows jump when she sees Landon shirtless, but I lounge against the counter like it's no big thing.

"McKenna accidentally dumped an entire cake on him," I explain, the picture of nonchalance. "I told him he could use our washer so the stain doesn't set."

Mark gives me a look that says he's onto us, but Mom's face softens.

"Oh, of course," she says as she boots Landon out of the way. "Here. Let me take care of it for you. Lacey was such a mess when she was younger. I can get out just about any stain you put in front of me."

Usually, I'd be irritated with her blabbing that kind of information, but now I'm so relieved, I only pretend to look embarrassed.

"Thanks, Mrs. Mo—" he cuts off when he sees the look on her face. "Cassie."

"It's no problem. You'll probably want to head back to your site before it gets too chilly. If you wait, you'll freeze."

If Landon's half as warm as I am, he'll be fine.

"I thought you were going to a movie," I say absently.

"Nothing was playing." Mark pulls out a chair at the table. He's still watching the two of us with suspicious eyes.

"That's too bad," I murmur, and I mean it with all my heart. Then I say to Mom, "I'm going to walk back with Landon."

"That's fine." Mom glances over her shoulder at my fake-but-starting-to-seem-real boyfriend. "Will you ask your mom if she wants to come over for coffee tomorrow morning before we go into town?"

"Will do," Landon promises.

We say our goodbyes, and I breathe a great big sigh of relief as soon as we're out the door. We walk a few yards before I peek at Landon. "Are you cold?"

He gives me a sideways look, smiling in a satisfied sort of way. "No. You?"

"I'm good."

"Do you think your mom noticed the chocolate in your hair?" His smile grows just the tiniest bit wicked.

Frantic, I raise a hand to my head. It must have smeared on me when we were...doing what we were doing.

"Oh my goodness," I say, groaning. No wonder Mark was looking at us like that.

Landon laughs and wraps an arm around my waist, pulling me to his side as we walk. A breeze blows through the trees, and he holds me tighter, feigning a dramatic shiver.

"Cold?" I ask, snuggling next to him with the excuse of keeping him warm—it's bad business to let our campers freeze to death after all.

"Frigid," he bluffs, meeting my eyes. Then there's another cool breeze, and he shudders for real. "Okay, that's actually pretty cold."

I laugh as we continue to his campsite.

"COULD the two of you be any cuter?" Paige demands.

I shift my phone and continue watering the planter in front of me. If I move even a foot, my cell will drop the call. The petunias are about to do the backstroke, but I don't care because Landon's weaseled his way into my life and become my very favorite topic of conversation.

"And have you read the comments they got on that last video? You're public enemy number one for a whole group of girls who were hoping Landon would fall in love with them."

I stay away from the comments. It's better that way.

"This is the part where you admit to your best friend that you're head over heels for him," she coaxes.

Not happening. If I say it out loud...well, then I've said it out loud. And you can't take that sort of thing back.

No matter how true it might be.

I'm doomed.

"We're excellent actors," I hedge. "Seriously, I should make a career out of it."

"Liar," she says with a laugh. "You are so gone for him."

I roll my eyes. This is why you shouldn't have best friends—they know you too well.

"Oh!" Paige exclaims suddenly. "I think Tanner's here. I have to get the door before Trenton."

"Why exactly do you have to beat your brother to the front door?" I ask.

"He doesn't care for Tanner."

"*Really.*"

"Stop. You know very well none of my brothers have ever liked anyone I've dated."

Which tells you the stellar taste Paige has in guys.

"Best hurry then," I tease. "Run little rabbit, beat your brother to the door."

"Bye!" she chirps, and then she's gone.

"Ladybugs are our friends." Landon comes up behind me and pulls me into a hug, surprising me. "And we shouldn't drown our friends."

Sure enough, a poor little rosy, spotted beetle is fighting for its life, clinging to a leaf that's hanging in the pool of water I created.

I shoot Landon a look over my shoulder and free myself from his arms so I can move the insect to safer territory.

"Hi," he says when I look back, his light green eyes

bright. Spring eyes, that's what they are. The color of soft, new grass and inviting meadows.

Knock it off, Lacey.

"Hi." I slip my phone into my pocket and tug the hose down to the next barrel.

Landon follows me. "Any reason in particular you felt the need to make a swamp in that barrel?"

"I was talking to Paige."

"That doesn't make a lot of sense."

"Did you come to criticize my gardening skills, or did you need something?"

"Mostly, I came to criticize your gardening skills."

He leaps back when I point the hose at him and use my thumb to direct the spray. Recovering from his surprise quickly, he darts forward, soaking wet, trying to wrestle the hose from me.

"No!" I yelp, laughing as he manages to point it right at me. The water is *cold.*

A car slowly makes its way down the road, and we immediately stop, afraid we'll spray it instead of each other. A man about my uncle's age scowls at us as he rolls down the window. "That's an irresponsible use of water."

"Sorry," I say, biting back a different sort of response.

Landon nods, looking contrite.

With a beady-eyed glare, the man continues.

Landon glances at me once the camper is out of earshot, trying not to smirk. "See that? You got us in trouble."

I shoot him a look.

He leans close. "Imagine how horrified he would be if

he knew you tried to murder a ladybug—one of the most beneficial of the garden insects."

Before I go back to my chore, I point the hose at him again—just for a moment. "Go away."

He holds up his hands, grinning as water drips from his chin. "Want to go into town and try out the miniature golf course after you get done working?"

"It's pretty run down."

"So that's a yes?"

I go back to watering the flowers instead of Landon and grin because my back is toward him. "Yes."

CHAPTER EIGHTEEN

"IS IT REAL GOLD?" Caleb asks, skeptical of my activity. He narrows his eyes at the sand-filled kiddie pool.

"No, but it kind of looks like gold," I tell him.

"And you can trade it in for prizes when we're finished," Landon adds.

That's enough to convince Caleb to grab a sand sifter and join the other kids, and I shoot Landon a grateful look.

Our barbecue is in full swing. We've had a record turnout this year. Even people staying at the state park and hotels in town have stopped by. Uncle Mark's grilling hot dogs, sausage, and hamburgers, and Mom's cutting up watermelon and refilling massive platters. We always pick a charity to donate the money to, and this year it's going to the new park and playground Gray Jay wants to build at the edge of Main.

A little girl squeals when she finds her first piece of treasure, and Caleb promptly tells her it's not real gold.

"Caleb," Landon warns. His brother looks over, giving him a *"well, it's not"* look, and goes back to sifting sand.

Despite himself, Caleb hollers with joy when he finds his first piece.

Landon rolls his eyes, but he's smiling. Everyone is in good spirits. We've had enough rain in the last few days that the town's fire department has decided it's safe to set off the fireworks we had to skip on the Fourth of July, so it's the first year out of several that we will get a display. The barbecue wraps up around five, and then we're headed over to the lake. Mrs. Tillman and Mom have been hanging out together all afternoon, and it seems they've decided we're going to sit together.

I catch them flashing Landon and me indulgent looks, and that familiar feeling of guilt squeezes my chest. It didn't seem like a big deal in the beginning, but now our fake relationship feels like exactly what it is—a lie.

Or is it?

This is why "It's complicated" has become an official relationship status.

"Your brother is smiling," I tell Landon, nodding toward the gazebo. Hunter sits with a pretty girl about his age. They both eat popsicles that Uncle Mark brought out in a huge cooler about fifteen minutes ago.

Landon pulls his phone from his pocket and snaps a picture. Then he grins at me. "Got to document these rare Happy Hunter sightings."

A little later, when we're cleaning up the gold mining activity, Paige shows up.

"Perfect timing," I tell her. "Grab a side."

Silent and obedient, she grabs a side of the kiddie pool and helps Landon and me drag the whole thing behind the office. I glance at her, instantly aware something is wrong.

Landon must sense it too. "I'm going to check on Caleb," he says, "just to make sure he's keeping himself out of trouble."

I wait until Landon's away before I turn to Paige. "What's wrong?"

"Nothing," she says, but she won't meet my eyes.

"Come on. I know you better than that."

She crosses her arms, and I realize she's not wearing any makeup, and her shirt is one of her brother's oversized T-shirts. She hasn't dressed like this since she was fourteen.

"Tanner wasn't as wonderful as I thought," she finally admits.

"What did he do?" I ask, ready to hunt him down and make him hurt even though I don't know what happened.

She rubs the bridge of her nose, acting like she has an itch. With the way her eyes glisten, I'm afraid she's trying not to cry. "I'm so stupid."

"You're not stupid," I say immediately, though I'm starting to get nervous. What happened?

Her face crumples, and she blinks quickly as several tears run down her cheeks. "I thought he liked me—like, really liked me. Then he just stopped calling, and this morning he admitted he has a *girlfriend*."

I suck in a breath. It's just like Thomas all over again.

"He said he feels guilty, and that he loves her, and he can't see me anymore."

I stare at her, genuinely hurting for her.

"You were right," she says, wiping away tears. "You can't trust summer boys. I was an idiot."

"No." I hug her, feeling ready to cry myself. I know exactly how she feels right now, and I hate that she's hurting. "This isn't your fault. He led you on and lied to you —this is all on him."

"It feels like my fault," she says with a sniff. "I let him get too close."

"It's going to be okay," I tell her, and I mean it. "We all make mistakes—give our hearts to people who don't deserve them, do things we wish we could take back. But soon it won't hurt so much."

She nods and pulls away, gaining control of her tears. "I should have listened to you when you said you didn't like him."

"I don't think I ever said it."

She gives me a dry look. "Please. It was written all over your face."

That's probably true.

"Are you going to the fireworks?" she asks, needing to change the subject.

"Yep. You want to sit with us?"

"I don't think I'm going to go."

"There haven't been fireworks in three years. You *have* to come."

"Maybe," she says, but I don't think she's going to make it.

"Do you want me to stay home with you?" I ask. "We could do a sleepover, watch movies or something?"

She shakes her head. "No, you have to go. Aren't you supposed to hang out with Landon?"

I groan and rub my hands over my face. I'm not sure this is the best time to talk to her about all this.

"You like him, don't you?" she prods, probably ready to deal with someone else's problems.

"*So much.*" I finally admit.

"You know that's okay, don't you? He's not Thomas." She scowls. "He's not Tanner either."

"No more T-names," I joke.

"Deal."

We fall silent. Summertime sounds drift our way— children laughing, people chatting, birds making racket in the trees.

"I think I'm going to head home," Paige says after another moment. "I look awful."

"You're too pretty to ever look awful," I argue.

"Thanks." She gives me a small smile. "Go to the fireworks tonight. Tell Landon how you feel—stop pretending and make it real."

"You just made a rhyme."

She rolls her eyes. "Promise? I can see you're miserable."

"I'll think about it."

"What are you so scared of? You already know he doesn't have a girlfriend."

I look up at a big, fluffy white cloud floating across

the sky. "He's going to leave, keep traveling, eventually go off to college."

"So? We graduate next year. What's keeping you here?"

I give her an incredulous look. "I don't know—everything? You know Mom needs me. She and Mark can't run this place on their own."

Paige looks like she wants to argue, but she finally nods. "You're smart. You'll figure it out."

"Hey, Paige," I call as she walks away.

She turns back.

"You're going to be okay. I promise."

Biting her bottom lip to keep from crying, she nods and then moves on. I hug myself, aching for her. I remember. *Oh, I remember*.

Landon finds me a bit later. "Everything okay?"

I step into him, wrapping my arms around his middle. "Yeah."

He sets one hand on my back and runs the other down my hair. "You positive? Because I'm pretty sure you're crying."

And he's right, but these few escaped tears aren't for Thomas. Though all of this has dredged up a slew of memories I'd rather stayed buried, my tears are for Paige —because her pain is a mirror of mine a year ago. I can identify with it too easily, feel it, even taste the betrayal. I hate that Tanner did this to her.

"Why do people cheat?" I ask, looking up to meet Landon's eyes.

His face softens, and I know he's put the pieces

together and figured out why Paige was so upset. "Because they're selfish."

Our situations were different. His girlfriend cheated on him, and Paige and I were used. But it's all the same really.

"Hey, Lacey?" he says after a moment.

I look back at him.

His hand slowly moves on my back, rubbing gentle circles. "You know that if we were together—really, truly together, even if we were states apart, I would never do that to you, right?"

My heart swells, and I give him a watery smile. "Hypothetically speaking?"

His solemn expression softens. "Yeah."

I set my cheek on his chest, listening to the steady thrum of his heart. "Yes, I do know that."

And I mean it. The problem is, we're not really, truly together, are we?

———

IT'S JUST GETTING DUSKY, and we've found the perfect spot to park. Mom and Mrs. Tillman pass out sodas and snacks, and Caleb and McKenna run around Uncle Mark's truck, waving glow sticks that it's not quite dark enough for.

Landon sits next to me in the bed of the truck. Everyone else is in lawn chairs, but we're on Mark's diamond plate toolbox next to the back window.

We're sitting here, laughing at Caleb and McKenna,

when Landon's phone rings. Surprised to see he has service, he pulls it out of his pocket and then sighs when he sees the number. Immediately, he silences it.

I don't even have to ask to know who it is.

Without a word, Landon sets his arm around my shoulders, drawing me to his side.

Then his phone rings again. This time, he dismisses the call and turns the phone off.

"I'm sorry," he says.

I shrug, not knowing how I feel. He and Evie were together for three years after all—he must still care for her, at least a little bit. Even if he doesn't want to. Even if *I* don't want him to.

When Mrs. Tillman's phone rings, I get the first premonition that something is amiss. She frowns and turns to Landon. "Any idea why Evie is calling me?"

Landon holds his hands out, wordlessly telling her he has no idea and doesn't really want to know.

Mrs. Tillman looks down at the number, conflicted. "Do you think everything's all right with her parents? It seems strange she'd call me if it wasn't an emergency."

And then, because she's a mom and she just can't help herself, she answers the phone. "Hi, Evie," she says in a warm but cautious tone—one that makes me realize she knew Landon's ex pretty well.

"Oh," Mrs. Tillman says, her eyes getting huge. "I...well."

A mask falls over Landon's face, and he stares at his mother.

"We're at the fireworks right now, but we'll be back at

the—" Mrs. Tillman stops abruptly like she was interrupted. She flashes Landon a helpless look and shakes her
head, like whatever is happening is completely out of her
control. "I'm not sure that's the best idea."

I tug away from Landon and draw my knees to my
chest, crossing my arms over them.

"No, I don't think it's smart to drive back in the
dark..." Mrs. Tillman turns her face toward the sky.
"We're near the lake, not far from the boat ramp."

She's here. Evie is *here.*

How is this even happening?

"Mom," Landon practically snarls as soon as Mrs.
Tillman hangs up the phone.

She shakes her head, looking incredibly uncomfortable. "I didn't know what to do. She said she drove here to
see you. I didn't want to send her back this late."

"From home?" Landon asks, incredulous. "That's at
least fifteen hours."

So...apparently Evie is unbalanced. That's good to
know—I'll just file that tidbit of information away.

"I'm so sorry, Lacey," Mrs. Tillman says, turning to
me. She grimaces, looking mildly dazed. Apparently, she
didn't know Evie was insane either.

Mom and Uncle Mark don't say anything, but I can
tell they're questioning the wisdom of pushing my relationship with Landon.

"How can she just drive here?" I demand to no one in
particular.

"She's eighteen," Landon says quietly. "Same as me.
If she wants to hop in the car and drive fifteen hours to

confront her ex-boyfriend, there's not much stopping her."

She's older than me. Even better.

Twenty minutes later, a dark green sedan drives slowly through the line of cars, and it stops when it reaches the Tillman's Suburban.

"Is that her?" I ask Landon at a whisper.

He gives me a tight nod.

There's not a lot of room between the SUV and the truck on the other side of them, but Evie manages to maneuver into it.

I sit here, more uncomfortable than I've ever been in my life, waiting for the first glimpse of the girl Landon was in love with.

And then there she is. Does she look insane? *No*, she looks gorgeous. Her hair is a medium brunette shade, and it falls in a perfectly straight sheet to her waist. She has perfect cheekbones, light eyes framed with long lashes, and she's slender and tall like a model.

And she doesn't look eighteen—she looks twenty.

She glances my way and then dismisses me like I'm nothing more than an insignificant speed bump in her plan to win Landon back.

"Landon," she says, her eyes finding his. It's a greeting, reprimand, and a purr all at once. "We need to talk."

He glances at our group. Every single one of us, except for Caleb who couldn't care less, watches the two of them.

Looking plenty uncomfortable, Landon gives her a curt nod. Then he turns to me. "I will be right back."

I try to smile, but it's weak at best.

Landon leaps from the truck, and as he steers her away from the group, I try not to admire how good they look together. They look like they stepped off the cover of a summer-themed magazine, one that makes teens everywhere feel inadequate.

I sit with a forced smile on my face, waiting, waiting, waiting for Landon to return. I refuse to look at my phone to check the time, but it's been at least fifteen minutes since Evie stole him away, maybe more.

"Oh, I forgot your lemon tea," I absently hear Mom say to Uncle Mark.

I leap to my feet. "I'll go back for it."

Mark shoots me a concerned look. "It's not a big deal. I'll drink a soda."

"No, I got it." I don't wait for a reply before I hop out of the truck. As I'm hurrying away, back toward our campground that's a good thirty-minute walk from here, I hear Mom call my name.

I keep going. As soon as I reach the main road, I start to run. I make it back in record time, but even when I catch my breath, I still can't *breathe*.

Why did I let my guard down? I *knew* better.

I stop in front of the fish pond, staring at the dark water, ruminating over my rotten life choices. At least I didn't tell Landon I wanted to stop pretending.

That would make it all that much worse. The last thing I need is him to pity me.

Poor little campground girl. She went and fell for one of the guests.

It's almost dark now, and the campground lights have flickered to life. The fireworks will start soon, but I don't intend to go back.

Mom and Uncle Mark will understand.

The campground is so quiet you can hear the creek bubbling just past Hallie and Greg's cabin. Most of the campers are in the grassy meadow by the lake, waiting for the display to start.

A dog barks from one of the sites, and then he goes silent. Everything is so still; it's a little eerie.

I head for the house, knowing I'll feel better once I'm inside. Just as I round the corner, I hear the crunch of rapidly approaching footsteps on the gravel behind me. My heart freezes. I whirl around and find a shadowed figure heading my way.

I let out a yip and stumble back, ready to dart.

"It's me," Landon says, finally close enough I can make him out in the dim glow of our front porch light. He sets his hands on his hips and draws in a deep breath. "You're fast when you're not in flip-flops."

"What are you doing here?" I will my heart to return to a regular pace, but it's still racing like a spooked rabbit.

He steps forward in the dark. "Your mom said you left. I came looking for you."

I don't know how to answer. I realize I showed him my cards—he knows how I feel about him now that I ran away from the fireworks. Why else would I care that he went off with Evie?

Speaking of his psycho ex-girlfriend...

"Where's Evie?" I ask.

"Watching the fireworks, I guess."

"Didn't she care that you left?"

A smile toys at his lips. "She was livid, but not because of the fireworks."

I study him, wondering why he's here. Unless, maybe, just maybe, this thing I'm feeling is mutual.

"I'm sorry," I whisper. "I know she hurt you, and it had to have been hard to see her again."

He steps forward, meeting me. "It wasn't so bad, not with you there."

My stomach does a flip when he says almost the same thing I said to him about Thomas.

Not too far away, the first firework cracks in the sky. Though it's masked by the nearby trees, the boom is still impressive.

"I have an idea," Landon says suddenly, grabbing my hand and leading me to the side of the house.

"Where are we going?"

He stops at a ladder Mark has propped against the house. He was using it to fix a piece of trim this week, and he never got around to finishing.

"Ever climbed onto the roof?" Landon asks, jerking his chin toward the ladder.

"No," I laugh.

"Do you want to?"

I look at the ladder and then back at Landon. Instead of answering, I check to see if it's sturdy, and then I begin my climb. Landon stays at the bottom, holding the ladder until I reach the top.

"Who's going to hold it for you?" I ask.

"I'll be careful."

I wait for him at the top, stepping back when he reaches me. The roof isn't steep, nor is this section very high.

Landon takes my hand and leads me to a spot near the ridge. "How's this?" he asks.

We can just see the fireworks over the tall trees, and we have the sky to ourselves.

"It's perfect."

We sit side by side, the tips of our fingers brushing, and watch the show. After a few minutes, Landon looks my way.

"Yes?" I ask, my focus still on the fireworks though my attention is solely on Landon.

"I like you," he says, a sentiment that demands I look his way.

He continues, "I liked you the moment you tripped over your chair when you were leaving your desk to show me to the campsite."

My stomach warms and tightens, but my limbs are loose and languid.

"I like you too," I say even though I'm scared and elated and a dozen emotions in between.

"Then why don't we stop ignoring this is happening when we both know it is? I'm not with you because I want to make my family happy. I'm with you because *you* make *me* happy."

"And Evie?" I ask because I must know.

"Evie does not make me happy," he says firmly.

I set my hand over his, and he immediately turns it so

our palms meet.

"You could leave anytime now," I point out. "What if your parents decide they're done with Gray Jay? That they want to move on early?"

He digs his phone out of his pocket and holds it up. "There's this really awesome device. It's called a phone. We can each use one and talk no matter where we are in the country."

I shake my head. "It's not the same, and you know it."

"Day by day, Lacey. I don't know where we'll be in a year, but I know I'm here, right now, with you. And I don't want to waste it."

Almost every fiber of my being wants to give in and see where this goes. But the part of me that was hurt by Thomas fights. I'm stuck here. I'll *always* be stuck here because this is where my family needs me. This might be fun now, but what about in a month? The summer can't last forever.

Seeing the conflict written on my face, Landon strokes my hand with his thumb.

"Everyone leaves," I say quietly, looking down at our hands. "They come through, stay just long enough I get attached, and then they move on with their lives while I stay here, stagnant."

He waits, letting me get my thoughts in order.

"I want this." I squeeze his hand as I look up. "But I'm afraid if we go there, if we make this real, it's going to destroy me when you go."

"Then let's not put labels on it. We won't make it

'official'—you won't be my fake girlfriend or my real girl-friend. You'll just be my Lacey."

And my heart nearly breaks right now because the way he says it makes it sound infinitely sweeter than any official label.

Sighing in resignation, I lean my head against his shoulder and nod.

Relaxing, he pulls his hand from mine and loops his arm around my shoulders. We continue to watch the fire-works. They light the sky, coming faster now as the finale begins.

He shifts just a little, turning his head so he's facing me instead of the sky.

"*What?*" I ask, trying not to smile.

"I'm wondering if I can kiss you. Is that allowed with our new arrangement?"

"No," I say, being difficult just because I can.

Landon waits, probably trying to figure out if I'm serious.

Laughing under my breath, I turn into him, set my hand on his shoulder to anchor myself so I don't fall off the roof, and press my lips to his.

CHAPTER NINETEEN

WITHOUT HESITATION, Landon meets me. It's a sweet kiss—not searing like the one in the kitchen or new and exciting like the one in the barn—sweet. The kind that's interrupted by smiles.

But through it all, the little voice in the back of my head warns me to think about the consequences of falling for another summer boy.

I shift back after a moment so I can meet Landon's eyes. "Just this one time, understand?"

"Just this?" he asks, incredulous, raising his voice so I can hear him over the cracks and booms of the last of the firework display.

I nod.

He sets his forehead against mine and closes his eyes, smiling in a way that makes me think he's wondering how he found such a difficult girl.

After a moment, he opens his eyes and meets my gaze. "Then let's make it memorable."

He slides his hand along the base of my neck, bringing me closer, and our mouths meet again. The sky quiets, and the kiss deepens.

When the first car lights shine through the trees, alerting us people will be arriving back at the campground soon, Landon breaks the kiss. "I suppose we should climb down before everyone gets here."

I nod.

He presses one last soft, short kiss to my lips and then we carefully make our way to the ladder. The only problem is...the ladder's on the ground.

We stare down at it.

"That's inconvenient," Landon finally says, looking at me.

We hold each other's gaze for several full seconds before laughter bubbles up inside of me, and I can no longer contain it. Landon grins, chuckling himself.

"Might as well sit." Landon lowers himself to the edge of the roof. I join him, and we dangle our legs over the edge while we wait for Mom and Uncle Mark to show up.

"What's your mom going to think about us watching the fireworks from the roof?" Landon asks as Uncle Mark's truck pulls into the drive.

"Honestly? I have no idea."

"Well, we're about to find out."

As soon as they're out of the truck, we wave our hands and call out to get their attention. Mom looks over, startled.

"Lacey Harriet Adele! What are you doing on the roof?"

Both middle names? She's not happy.

"Harriet Adele?" Landon teases quietly.

I gently elbow him in the ribs as I holler back, "We were watching the fireworks, but the ladder fell while we were up here."

Uncle Mark grins and walks below us, craning his neck to look up. "How do you plan to get down?"

I set my hands on my hips. "You're going to hand us that ladder."

"I am?" he teases. Thankfully, he's more amused than my mother.

After a few more minutes of joking, he finally sets the ladder against the house and holds it so we can climb down.

"Goodnight, Landon," Mom says, but it really means, "You're in trouble, Landon. Go back to your camper."

He gives her a sheepish grin. "Night, Mrs. Mor—Cassie. Night, Mark." Before he goes, he turns back to me and mouths, "Goodnight, Lacey."

It warms me all the way to the tips of my toes.

"Bye," I mouth back.

At least Mom waits until he's gone before the scolding begins. "The roof, Lacey? In the dark? Do you know how dangerous that is?"

"Oh, it's not that big of a deal," Mark says gently. "She's fine."

Mom scowls at him, but she finally gives in. Turning back to me, she says, "Don't do it again."

"Yes, Ma'am," I swear.

Before we go inside, I glance toward the campground. "What happened with Evie?"

Mom rolls her eyes. "Sarah put her up in a hotel in town and told her to drive home tomorrow. Landon's made it very clear he doesn't want her here."

Satisfied, I nod and head toward the house.

"How well could you see the fireworks from up there?" Uncle Mark asks.

I glance at Mom before I hide a smile and say, "Pretty well."

I don't think I need to admit I didn't watch most of them.

Uncle Mark grins at my mother. "Maybe we should all climb up there next year?"

She laughs and gives him a good, hard shove to the arm. "Not on your life."

———

"WHAT DID THAT ART CURATOR WANT?" I finally remember to ask Mom as we're making dinner several weeks after the man showed up. With everything going on with Landon, I forgot to ask.

She chops bell peppers to add to the onions already sautéing in the skillet. "He wants to show some of my work in his gallery."

"So...did he take anything?"

The peppers hiss and spit as she adds them to the hot

skillet. "He took a few pieces on consignment and said he'd see how much interest they garner."

"That's good, right? You're excited?"

She shrugs, snacking on a leftover piece of bell pepper. "I don't know if anything will come of it."

What she really means is she doesn't want to get her hopes up.

"Your stuff is amazing," I tell her. "It deserves to be in galleries...not coffee shops."

"It was very kind of Betta to let me display a few pieces," Mom reminds me almost sternly.

I nod, feeling adequately chastised, and stir rice and cooked sausage in with the peppers and onions. The conversation drops off as I finish preparing the jambalaya so it can cook.

"So...how are things going with Landon?" Mom asks smugly just as I'm putting the lid on the pot and turning down the temperature to a simmer.

That, Mother Dearest, is an excellent question.

"Fine."

She crosses her arms, smiling in a way that makes me want to avoid the question. "Just fine?"

"We're great, okay? Landon's great."

The scary thing is I mean it with my whole heart. Landon *is* great...and we're pretty great together. Too bad our poor relationship—or whatever you want to call it—is doomed. Star-crossed lovers and all that.

"He seems sweet," she says, getting all gooey and mom-ish on me. "And his family is wonderful."

Yes, I *know*. It's like she's insistent on rubbing lemon

juice on a wound—and she doesn't even know she's doing it.

Why couldn't our mothers see this was a bad idea?

Probably because teenagers don't actually fall in love, right? Like Paige said, you have to date several guys before you end up with the right one.

But what if you find him early?

Does that mean you don't get to keep him because the timing is all wrong? If so, that's a pretty crummy love story.

CHAPTER TWENTY

"I'M THINKING TOMORROW," Landon says, leaning over the counter, watching me work. He has his camera trained on me, but I hardly even notice anymore.

"Tomorrow what?" I drum my fingers next to my keyboard, looking at a map of the property, trying to decide if we could construct a dog run near the creek. I bet we could squeeze one in.

"Tomorrow, we're going to drive to Glenwood Springs and go on that date I promised your mom I'd take you on," he answers.

"I have to prune the roses next to the fishpond."

"Do it Monday, and I'll help you."

I give him a look, but that only makes him grin. He turns the camera so it's focused on his face. "Lacey says she doesn't have time, but I think I can talk her into it."

"I can't take you seriously when you're talking to your imaginary friends," I tease him.

"I'm very serious," he insists, shutting off the camera.

"We'll leave in the morning, explore a little, have an early dinner, and head back."

"Glenwood is about four hours away."

"Humor me."

"Where exactly do you intend to explore?"

He flips out a brochure of a cave tour. "Cool, right?"

Absolutely, except for one tiny problem—I'm terribly claustrophobic, and caves are creepy. "You are not getting me in there."

He rests both elbows on the counter and leans down, giving me a pleading look that he full well knows is addictive. "Come on. It'll be fun. And I need something new for the channel—we're running out of material around here."

Now *that* worries me because it might mean his parents are ready to move on.

I look at the brochure again. It shows smiling families in a cavern filled with soft, ambient light. Never mind that the stalactites look like giant dripping fangs.

"Say yes," Landon coaxes.

Closing my eyes, I groan. "All right. If you really have your heart set on it."

"I do," he assures me.

"And you have to help me with the roses."

He taps the brochure on the table, grinning like a little boy who got away with something. "There's nothing I enjoy more."

"Except for guided cave tours," I point out.

With a wink, he walks backward toward the door and agrees, "Except for cave tours."

"You want to help construct a dog run too? A two for one sort of thing?"

Uncle Mark walks into the office, hearing the last of the conversation. "Where in the world would you put in a dog run?"

"Near the creek, by Cabin Four."

Mark shakes his head, chuckling. "You're giving a hundred and ten percent, Lacey my love. Feel free to back it down to a hundred. Heck, you're a teenager—we'd be happy with eighty."

Landon laughs but holds his hands up in surrender when I shoot him a look.

Mark turns to Landon, still joking. "If it were up to my niece, we'd work every minute of the day, and only sleep six hours at night."

I roll my eyes and go back to looking at the map, already searching for a better location for the dog run.

"Are you two going to the concert in the park tonight?" Mark asks as he shuffles through a drawer, probably looking for the licorice I finished a few days ago.

"Are we?" I ask Landon and then turn back to my uncle. "What is it tonight?"

"Some instrumental thing," he says, wrinkling his nose. Classical's not exactly his cup of tea.

I give Landon a questioning look, and he shrugs. "If you want to."

Might as well. It's not like there's anything else going on in Gray Jay. "Sure. I'll be here until six—"

"Wait, weren't you supposed to have the day off?" Mark interrupts.

"I'll be done at *six*," I continue, giving Mark a stern look before I turn back to Landon. "I'll come find you after."

Landon nods as he opens the door. Pausing over the threshold, he turns the camera back on. "Told you," he says in a voice that's cocky yet somehow irresistible. "She said yes to the caves."

"But you have to help prune roses on Monday!" I remind him before he's out the door.

"And I have to prune roses on Monday," he tells the camera, making me smile as he leaves.

CHAPTER TWENTY-ONE

UNBEKNOWNST TO UNCLE MARK, and much to his chagrin, Mom and Mrs. Tillman already planned a family outing to tonight's concert before he mentioned it to Landon and me earlier. He's now stuck here with us, listening to violins, violas, and that big stringed instrument that's too big to hold.

He fell asleep five minutes ago, stretched out on a picnic blanket. Candy is intrigued by his light, whistling snores. Every time he inhales, she inches a tiny bit closer and then jumps back when he breathes out. She's standing over him now, one paw extended, looking like she's ready to smack him on the nose.

I wait, enjoying this particular show more than the music.

The quartet announces they're going to take a small intermission, and they exit the stage.

Immediately, as if he's been waiting all this time,

Caleb plops onto the grass in front of us and unfolds a map. "Look what I found."

It's a local trail map, and I recognize most of the areas he has circled. The one he points to is the shanty Landon and I took him to at the beginning of the summer.

"Hey, good map reading skills," Landon says.

Caleb beams, and he points to another spot not far away. "Look at what this says."

"Prospector's Demise," I say, knowing what it is but waiting for him to tell me because he's so excited.

"Demise means death, right?" Caleb says, excited.

"In this case."

"This is where Gideon Bonavit went off the cliff with his gold!"

I nod. "It's the spot they *think* he went off. It happened so long ago. No one really knows for sure."

Excited, he points to several more circled locations on the map, all nearby places where gold was mined.

"I copied them from the map in the book. Isn't it cool?" He gives us a big, hopeful grin. "Maybe we can go for a drive tomorrow? Check some of them out? There's gotta be gold *somewhere*."

I glance at Landon, not wanting to be the one to tell Caleb we're not going to be here.

"Hey, bud, Lacey and I are going on a short day trip tomorrow," Landon says gently. "Maybe we can try for next weekend."

"Oh...okay." Caleb's face falls, and he carefully folds up his map. He looks back up, a spark of hope still in his eyes. "You promise?"

Landon glances at me, and I nod. Mom won't mind if I take another Saturday off. Honestly, I could probably take the rest of the summer, and Mom and Mark would be relieved I'm working on my social life. You'd think I was a hermit from the way those two talk.

Caleb grins and runs off, going who knows where.

"Thank you for humoring him," Landon says, tracing my hand with his finger.

I don't know what's going on between us exactly, but I'm happy, and I think he is too.

Paige appears behind us and nods to Mark. "I see your uncle is riveted by the show."

I turn, relieved to see her out. It's been two weeks since she discovered that Tanner's a toad, and she's spent most of that time at home.

"Hi," I say, scooting closer to Landon so she can sit next to me on our blanket. Nervous, I glance about. I saw Gia towing Thomas around earlier, so there's a good chance Tanner's here too.

"He's not here," Paige says, reading my mind.

"Are you sure?"

"I haven't seen him."

I frown, wondering if she *wants* to see him. But I know Paige too well to question that. Now that she knows he has a girlfriend, she won't touch him with a ten-foot pole.

"Did Trenton come with you?" I ask.

Her brother came home last weekend, and she told me on Wednesday they've been helping their dad with odd projects.

"Trenton is here with some girl he met yesterday. Dad's with Diane."

There was a time when we were younger that we thought her dad and my mom might get together, but it never came to pass. Now he's seeing a lady that works in the travel center. I'm not sure how Paige feels about it. My mom has never seemed interested in dating, so I have trouble picturing how awkward it would be.

"I'm going to grab something to drink, and then I'll be back," she promises.

I turn to Landon. "I'll go too. You want something?"

Sensing I need a little time with Paige, he hands me a five and asks for a soda. "I'm going to talk to the musicians," he adds. "See if they mind if I film a little of their performance."

Paige and I walk toward the food carts parked along the grass. They're all busy, so we pick the shortest line and wait.

"Brace yourself," Paige says when Gia, Thomas, Jarrett, and *Tanner* amble our way.

Tanner won't even look at Paige—guilt is written all across his face. But as always, Jarrett can't look at anyone else. There are questions in his eyes, concern. But I barely notice the sweet way he studies my friend because *Thomas* is looking at *me*.

"Hey," Thomas says when their group joins us at the back of the line.

Gia frowns, not liking the attention Thomas is showing me. She sidles next to him and tries to slide her arm through his, but he subtly steps to the side, avoiding her. Apparently, despite how hard she's trying, they haven't gotten back together.

Anger and hurt flash in her eyes, but she tries to mask it.

"We need to talk, Lace," Thomas says, using the shortened version of my name like he did when we were together.

"We're good, Thomas," I say, and as soon as the words are out of my mouth, I realize I mean it. I've moved on, and I'm finally in a place where I can forgive him for how he hurt me. Even if he doesn't deserve it.

"But I'm not good," he says, stepping toward me, even farther away from Gia.

On instinct, Paige steps closer to my side, protecting me, showing him it's two against one should he push too hard.

"I miss you," he says, lowering his voice. People around us glance our way, curious.

Jarrett, uncomfortable, clears his throat.

"I just want to talk," Thomas pleads.

Gia crosses her arms, glaring at me—like this is somehow my fault.

"I'm with Landon now," I tell Thomas firmly. "What happened between us last summer is done. Finished. That's all there is to it."

Thomas starts to argue, but Jarrett steps forward. "Enough, Thomas. Leave her alone."

"Why do you care?" Thomas says, shaking Jarrett off. "You don't want her. You're too enamored with her easy friend."

Gia's mouth drops open, and Paige sucks in a gasp. Tanner's eyes go wide, and he looks around, almost as if he's planning his escape. Slowly, like a viper, Paige turns to face Tanner. "What exactly have you been telling people?"

He holds up his hands, shaking his head, looking guilty, guilty, guilty.

And then the strangest thing happens. Calm, quiet, sweet Jarrett turns on Tanner. With narrowed eyes and a deadly calm tone, he demands, "What *have* you been telling people, Tanner?"

"Oh, come on," Tanner says to Jarrett, desperate to defend himself. "It's not like everyone doesn't already think she's a—"

And before he can complete that horrific thought, Jarrett punches him.

Gasps break out around us as Tanner recovers from the initial shock and charges his cousin. The two boys end up on the ground. Paige and Gia scream at them to stop, but there's no need. They're already being pulled apart by several of the men who were standing nearby in the concession lines.

A crowd has gathered—gawkers eager to see what all the commotion is about. Blood runs from Tanner's lip, and the skin is broken by the side of Jarrett's eye. It's going to be black in the morning.

"What is going on here?" Paige's dad's big voice booms as he cuts through the crowd. People part for the sheriff, murmuring to themselves.

"What happened?" he demands.

Jarrett looks at the ground, and Tanner refuses to answer.

Paige, bravest girl I know, crosses her arms, defiantly raises her chin, and stares at Tanner. "He's been spreading rumors about me—crude, hurtful rumors. *Lies.*" She looks like she's about to slap Tanner...or maybe kick him while he's down, but she controls herself and turns to the bleeding boy who defended her. "So Jarrett punched him."

Paige's poor dad looks taken aback—and for good reason. Quickly masking his shock, he stares down the two boys. "Are you done?"

They nod, though Tanner still looks livid. Jarrett seems uncomfortable but determined—like he doesn't regret what he did and would do it again if he had to.

"Let them go," Officer Hilden says to the men holding the boys. Then, to Tanner and Jarrett, he adds, "You two go at it again, and I'm taking you in. Understand?"

They both give him curt nods.

"You okay?" he asks, turning to Paige.

Her lower lip trembles, probably from fury as much as humiliation, but she nods.

Before he goes, Paige's dad turns back to Tanner and points at him, his face deadly serious. "And *you* will stay away from my daughter."

Embarrassed and angry, Tanner shoves his way through the crowd. Thomas shoots me one more look, and then he follows with Gia on his heels.

Officer Hilden watches them, and then he

awkwardly pats Paige on the shoulder, past uncomfortable, and heads back to his spot on the grass.

"I'm going to get such a talking to tonight," Paige mutters. She turns to our crowd, waving them away like she's shooing sheep. "Show's over. Go on now."

Most everyone goes back to minding their own business, but they're probably still listening. It doesn't matter. Gossip is going to spread no matter what.

"You're bleeding," Paige says to Jarrett, frowning at his eye.

Jarrett shrugs.

"Come on." She takes his hand. "Let's get you cleaned up."

And I try really hard not to whoop for joy. She flashes me a knowing smile over her shoulder as she heads for the parking lot, reading my mind yet again. "I'll call you later, 'kay?"

I clasp my hands to my chest, elated that something good came out of this catastrophe. "Okay."

Paige rolls her eyes at my enthusiasm, but she's smiling despite everything, and I am over the moon happy for her.

I head back to our spot on the grass and sit next to Landon, who's already returned. He looks at my empty hands and gives me a crooked grin. "Did you forget something?"

Instead of answering, I press a firm and fast kiss to his lips.

"What was that for?" he asks. He's kept his promise, and we haven't kissed since the roof.

"Thank you for being one of the good ones." I set my head on his shoulder.

Landon chuckles under his breath, a bit baffled, and says after a moment, "You know, I'm still kind of thirsty."

Growling but not meaning it, I yank him up. "Come on then. You can stand in line with me this time. Just try not to punch anyone."

Without missing a beat, still unaware of what happened, he loops his arm around my shoulder and says, "I'll do my best, but I can't make any promises."

CHAPTER TWENTY-TWO

EVEN THOUGH IT'S a four-hour drive to Glenwood Springs, it goes by surprisingly quickly. I'm fine when we first leave Gray Jay, but by the time we're taking the exit for the small mountain city, I'm less so.

"Nervous?" Landon asks, glancing over with a grin. We took my Jeep, but I was happy to let him drive.

"No." I shake my head to emphasize my point.

"Are you sure?" he asks, smirking at my shaking leg. "Because you *look* a little nervous."

I turn to him. "Did you know that miners used to carry canaries with them when they were going through caverns?"

He shakes his head, still smiling.

"You're probably wondering why," I say, though he didn't ask and probably doesn't care. "If one keeled over, it meant there was toxic gas nearby, and it was time to get out of there."

"And yet another lovely story." He smirks. "You should consider writing children's books."

I crack a smile despite myself.

Landon pulls into the parking area, turns off the Jeep, and pivots in his seat, resting his arm on the wheel. "If this particular cavern was dangerous, I don't think they would allow people in there."

"What if someone has a heart attack or an allergic reaction or...breaks a leg in the middle of the tour? Then what?"

"Well, I'm assuming the first step would be getting them out of the cave."

I know I'm being ridiculous, but the thought of walking underground...with the cave walls closing in on me...

Panic rises in my chest.

Landon studies me for several minutes, and then his smile softens. "We don't have to do this, not if you don't want to."

"But you want to. You've been looking forward to it."

"I've been looking forward to spending the day with *you*. The caves are just a nice bonus."

I inhale slowly and then exhale through my nose, trying to calm myself. "I can do it."

"You sure?" He raises a questioning eyebrow as if he doesn't believe me.

"Yes."

"Do you want to get some lunch first?"

"No, I'll change my mind." I roll my head, stretching

my neck. "Let's get this over with. Forty-five minutes, right?"

"That's what the brochure says."

I softly close the door, on the edge of chickening out. As I'm giving myself yet another pep talk, Landon comes around the front of the vehicle, sets his hands on my shoulders, and presses me against the side of the Jeep. "Thank you for being brave," he murmurs.

Startled, I laugh. Or I try to laugh...I was hyperventilating before, and now my air's gone.

His mouth meets mine, the pressure of his lips just firm enough to make my knees tremble, and then he lets me go.

"You can't just sneak up on a girl and kiss her," I say lightly, holding his sides to catch my balance while pretending my entire world didn't just tilt on its axis.

He raises an eyebrow, giving me a wicked look. "I can when the girl does it to me the night before."

Well, there you go.

———

TWENTY-FIVE MINUTES LATER, we're in the caverns, and I'm breathing just fine. You know...mostly.

"You okay?" Landon asks, gently setting his hand on the small of my back.

I nod, focusing on the rock formations and colors, and ignoring the fact that the mountain is surrounding me.

"Just pretend you're a dwarf, mining away in your

mountain home," Landon teases quietly so the other people on the tour won't overhear him.

"Did you really just say that?" I whisper back.

I'm rewarded with a swift grin, and we hurry to catch up with the tour.

Even I can admit the caves are spectacular. They've added lighting, so it's not too dark, and it makes the different minerals easier to see. Parts of the cave are extremely moist, and we pass a pool of water. Just above it hangs dripping stalactites made of calcite.

Occasionally, when the passages grow narrow, I have to remind myself to breathe. Landon, however, is fascinated. He spoke ahead of time with the tour company, and they've allowed him to take footage of the cave for his family's channel.

We stop several times, and our guide tells us about specific minerals and rock formations. Every time, Landon finds a way to connect with me. Sometimes he pulls me next to him. Other times it's just a hand resting on my back or an arm around my shoulder.

It's so natural with Landon, so comfortable.

Before we go home, I'm going to tell him how I feel. That I'm ready to label this—us. I want to be his girlfriend. I want to hear him say it out loud.

And I know the Tillmans are going to leave at the end of the summer, but we'll deal with it then. At least we have now.

We reach the very last cave, and our guide thanks us for joining him for the tour. Before we rejoin the rest of the world, a few people ask questions, Landon included.

I stand here, feeling pretty proud of myself. The caves were interesting enough; I'm almost sad to reach the end.

Almost.

Just as we're stepping into the glorious Colorado sunshine, both Landon and I receive texts.

"No service in there," Landon says, nodding toward the mountain we just exited.

I glance at my phone. Paige wants to know if I was stolen away by Gollum.

Still alive, I write. *Call you later*.

When I look up, I see Landon's still staring at his phone. His expression is different. I can't place it because I don't think I've ever seen it before.

"What's wrong?" I ask.

A ball of ice forms in my belly, and it spreads through my veins, chilling me despite the hot day.

Landon pockets his phone. "It was my dad."

"Okay," I say, waiting for him to elaborate.

He stares at the mountains across the Colorado River, looking at the red hillside and deep-green pine trees that grow on it. "There's a big meet up and RV convention in California. This morning, someone invited us to speak at it."

I wrap my arms around myself. "When's the convention?"

But I already know it's soon from the look on his face.

Slowly, Landon drags his gaze from the mountains and meets my eyes. "It starts next weekend."

"Next *weekend?*" I ask, feeling like the air has been

knocked out of me. "Like seven days from today next weekend?"

Landon nods. "The first of August."

"And your parents want to go?"

Again, he nods.

I knew he'd leave—I never denied it, not even to myself. But I didn't think it would be *now*.

"When do you leave?"

"Wednesday."

"Are you going to come back when it's over?"

He looks away again, and his eyes are troubled. I've never seen him like this, not even when Evie showed up out of the blue. I don't like it.

"I don't know," he finally answers.

After that, we walk back to my Jeep, neither of us speaking. Landon doesn't start the engine right away. We both sit in our seats, staring forward, trapped in our own heads.

What a strange life he leads—always leaving, always saying goodbye. Maybe it's not so bad being stuck in Gray Jay.

But I'm lying to myself. If I could go with Landon, I would. I would love nothing more than to see the things he's seen, do the things he's done.

And though we just met, the idea of doing those things together is incredibly appealing.

But I still have a year of school, and Landon's leaving now. Not to mention the fact that I can't abandon Mom and Uncle Mark. They need me. I know they tease me, but I do so much for the campground.

Maybe they don't realize how hard it would be without me, but *I* know.

Landon finally turns the key, and we head back on the highway, toward home. It's earlier than we planned, and we still haven't eaten dinner, but Landon must feel as out of sorts as I do.

"Where are you going?" I ask when he takes a random exit.

He follows a few signs, and we end up parked in front of a hiking trail in National Forest.

"I could use some fresh air. What about you?" he asks.

I study him for a minute, memorizing the flecks in his pale green eyes and the way his dark blond hair just brushes the tips of his ears. He already needs another haircut. "Yeah."

As a last-minute thought, Landon grabs a water bottle and leads us onto the trail. Though it's now evening, there's still plenty of light left. With Daylight Savings, the sun doesn't set until nearly nine this time of year.

We take our time, talking little, until Landon spots a tall outcropping of granite. We veer off the path, making our way to the top, and dangle our legs over to watch the sun sink lower in the sky. It's a picture-perfect view of the mountains in the distance, but Landon doesn't take out his camera or his phone.

Eventually, he turns to me. "I'm not sorry I met you, even if we didn't have a lot of time together."

My heart shatters.

"Me too." I blink quickly.

Landon tugs me next to him, and together we watch the sunset. We have a long drive ahead of us, but I don't mind putting it off.

He doesn't try to kiss me. I don't try to kiss him. We just sit together, coexisting, soaking the moment in.

It's well after dusk by the time we finally make it back to the Jeep. Just as I'm unlocking the doors, Landon's cell phone rings.

"Hey, we're on our way back," Landon answers. "I know it's getting late—" Landon frowns. "What do you mean he's missing?"

I stand by the hood, growing worried because of the look on Landon's face.

"How long has he been gone?"

From the sound of it, George must have gotten out.

Landon rubs a hand over his face. "We're still about three hours away, but we're on our way. We'll hurry." Before he hangs up, he assures the caller on the other line, "Yes, I promise I'll drive the speed limit—we'll be careful."

"Who was it?" I ask. Though a dozen questions are on the tip of my tongue, I catch myself before I bombard him with all of them at once.

"My dad." Landon gets into the Jeep, and so do I. I don't know what's going on, but I know we need to get back. As I'm buckling up, Landon starts the engine and heads for the highway. "Caleb's missing."

CHAPTER TWENTY-THREE

THE DRIVE back to Gray Jay feels like it takes all night. True to his word, Landon doesn't speed, though I know it's killing him. Only his promise to his dad is making him follow the restrictions on the white signs dotting the road.

Every green, reflective mile marker we pass brings us closer to home, and hopefully closer to Caleb. I keep telling myself that we're going to pull in and they'll have already found him, and everyone will laugh that he wasn't actually lost, he was just digging through rocks somewhere in the campground and didn't hear people looking for him.

But I know it's not true because if they found him, Landon would receive another call. And his phone has been eerily silent.

What we do find when we pull in is chilling.

Landon's hands tighten on the steering wheel, and he swallows, probably trying to choke down his fear. Flashlights bob around the campground, making it look like we have a whole mess of adult-sized Halloween tricker treaters wandering the property. From the looks of it, lots of people have come to help with the search.

Several sheriffs' cars sit in the registration parking area, and a bunch of people are talking to Paige's dad, my mom included. Relief washes over her face when she spots the Jeep, and she holds up her hand in a somber greeting as Landon pulls around the back.

"We're back," he says into his phone, already talking to his parents, who are thankfully in cell range somewhere. "Where do you need me?"

I'm ripping off my buckle before we're even stopped, ready to join the search.

Landon hangs up the phone and turns to me. "Dad wants me to talk to the officers, find out where's the best place to go."

We hurry to join the group with my mom. As soon as she sees me, she pulls me into a tight hug. The porch lights cast harsh shadows. Her sweet, pixie-esque face looks almost haggard in her worry.

"How long has he been gone?" I ask as Landon talks to the officers.

Mom shakes her head. "We're not sure. Hunter was watching him, but he disappeared a few hours ago."

"He took George?" I overhear Landon say, his tone incredulous.

Paige's dad nods.

Even though the dog is lazy and scared of the dark, it makes me feel a tiny bit better that Caleb isn't completely alone out there.

"Where do you need us?" I ask Officer Hilden.

"Paige is with the other kids right now in the family's camper," he says to me. "They're awfully upset. They know you pretty well—why don't you give her a hand?"

I nod. Though disappointed I won't be joining the search, I'll go wherever I'm needed.

Then Paige's dad says to Landon, "We have another group of volunteers going out in a minute. We don't want anyone taking off alone, but you are welcome to join them."

Landon nods. He then reaches for me, pulls me into a tight hug, and follows Officer Hilden to several more officers, a few men I recognize from town, and Paige's brother Trenton.

Now that Landon's out of earshot, I turn to mom before I join Paige in the Tillman's camper. Lowering my voice, I ask, "They don't think he was kidnapped, do they?"

Her face crumples, but she quickly schools the sharp stab of fear. "We don't know for certain, but they don't think so at this time. He took his bike, backpack, that small tent they set up in front of their camper, and the *dog*. Right now, they're treating him like a runaway."

"Caleb wouldn't run away," I argue.

"No, but you and I both know there's a good chance he wandered."

And then it hits me where he's at, where he's gone off to, and my legs almost give out. I grab hold of my mother. "When did you say he left?"

"Probably about five hours now."

SHARI L. TAPSCOTT

Right after the Tillmans got the news that they were leaving.

"He's looking for gold," I whisper, horrified. Gone off to find those circles on his map that we promised we'd take him to next weekend. But they won't be here next weekend—they'll be in California.

"Landon!" I yell across the parking lot, racing away from Mom without any explanation.

The group he's with turns toward me.

"Caleb took his tent and backpack—he's gone exploring. He's looking for gold."

And thank goodness I know Paige's dad well because he doesn't look at me like I've lost my mind.

"We have rangers searching the nearby trails," Officer Hilden assures me.

"Can you radio them? Tell them to check out Gideon's shanty and a few of the local mines? We were supposed to take him back, but he just found out his family's leaving in a few days."

Officer Hilden steps to the side, pulling his radio off his belt. Immediately, he relays the information. I feel sick with worry and guilt. I promised I'd take Caleb next weekend...and then he found out there wouldn't be a next weekend. He looked so crushed yesterday, but he should know better than to take off by himself.

Satisfied I've given them all I can, I turn back to Landon. "I'm going to go keep McKenna and Hunter company."

"Thank you," he says, squeezing my hand.

"Be careful, okay?"

He nods.

"We'll find him," Paige's brother assures me.

Reluctant to leave, wishing I could search, I walk down the campground road, using my phone as a flashlight.

The first thing I notice when I near Site Twenty-nine is Caleb and McKenna's toys scattered on the rug in front of the door. It looks like Caleb tossed everything out of their play tent and just left it all lying there. I knock at the door, sending Candy into a frazzled, yapping rage.

"Who is it?" Paige hollers, not about to unlock it for just anyone.

"It's me."

With a click of a lock, the door flies open. "I'm so glad you're back."

Candy darts out of the camper, barking like a mad thing. Once she realizes it's me, the racket ceases, and she follows me inside.

McKenna's sitting on the couch, knees drawn up to her chest, eyes puffy, and face red from her tears.

Hunter's next to her, looking pale. He sits with a throw pillow clutched to his stomach. He's holding it so tightly, he looks like a toddler with a security blanket. My heart breaks for him.

I kneel in front of them, not quite sure how to handle the situation. "Hey, guys."

"Is Landon out there?" Hunter asks.

I nod, and Hunter clutches the pillow tighter, looking angry. "Dad won't let me join a team."

"It's all right. There are so many people out there—someone's bound to find him soon."

Hunter meets my gaze. His eyes glisten with unshed tears. "Did they tell you it's my fault? It is. I was supposed to be watching him."

"It's going to be okay."

He finally breaks down. Several tears escape his eyes, but he scrubs them away with the back of his wrist.

"He was *right there*," he says, choking back a sob.

As nice as it is to see Hunter acting like a human, I wish I could take away his worry and guilt. Paige lingers behind me, unsure how to help.

We end up putting on a bright and happy movie that no one watches. Thirty minutes later, we turn it off. No one's in the mood for chipper right now.

Finally, we urge the kids to go to bed.

Unnaturally obedient, they go into the bunkhouse without argument and crawl into their beds without bothering to change into pajamas.

"Can you bring me Goldie?" McKenna asks in a small voice.

I look around for a doll or stuffed toy.

"The cat." She holds out her arms, waiting for her.

Sensing she's being summoned, the yellow tabby hops off the table bench and leaps onto McKenna's lower bunk. The girl lies back, stroking the cat's fur as the uppity feline walks around her and tries to find a comfortable spot. Eventually, the cat curls up by the pillow, and McKenna's eyes flutter closed.

After another hour or so without news, Paige ends up

pulling out the jackknife couch that lowers into a bed, and we lie on it, side by side. I set my phone between it, and we both stare at it, waiting for updates. It's the worst sleepover ever.

Somehow, we all manage to find sleep, and I don't wake until I hear a key in the front door.

I jerk awake as the remaining three Tillmans walk inside. Behind them, the light of early dawn tints the sky periwinkle. Caleb's conspicuous absence makes it hard to breathe.

Paige and I sit up, immediately awake. I meet Landon's eyes, but he only shakes his head.

"Thank you for watching the kids, girls," Mrs. Tillman says. Her face is gaunt, and her usually stylish hair is pulled back in a clip. Half of it hangs around her face, looking lifeless and flat.

All three sport dark smudges under their eyes from a sleepless night spent searching.

"More volunteers have arrived," Mr. Tillman says, giving us an explanation I didn't dare ask for. "Officer Hilden told us to try to get some sleep while they have other people out looking."

"I don't want to sleep," Mrs. Tillman suddenly snaps. "Not when Caleb's still out there."

Paige and I excuse ourselves, knowing the family needs some alone time. We murmur our goodbyes, telling them to call us the moment they need us again.

Landon follows us out and closes the door softly behind him. His parents' raised voices reach us, but they're not arguing. They're frantic.

"I'm going to see if Dad or Trenton is still here," Paige tells us. "Maybe I can catch a ride home with one of them."

She walks down the campground road.

Birds are already chirping from the trees, and though the morning air is frigid, it looks like it will be a pleasant day. It all seems too surreal. How is Caleb just gone? He was here yesterday morning—everything was *normal* yesterday morning.

Landon opens his arms to me, and I step into them without question. I bury my face against his chest and wrap my arms around him, holding him as tightly as I can. He doesn't cry like Hunter, but I can sense he feels the guilt too. It's not our fault Caleb took off, but there's still all those "what ifs" floating around in our minds. What if we'd postponed our trip into Glenwood? What if we'd taken Caleb on his excursion?

He'd still be here.

"Are you going to try to get some sleep?" I finally ask him.

His head is bent down, his whole body curled in close to me, so his cheek rubs against my ear as he nods. "I want to be alert enough to look some more soon."

"I'm going to lie down too. Call me if you need me, okay? Or if you hear anything?"

Landon nods, and we part, him going into the camper to join his grieving family and me heading toward my house.

The front door is locked, so I round the back. Not

sure if Mom's trying to sleep, I'm quiet as I slip in and softly shut the door behind me.

I hear whispers coming from the front room—Mom and Mark. They sound serious, and I don't think it's the time to interrupt them. I tiptoe past, hoping to slip into my bedroom undetected. But I freeze when I catch a glimpse of them.

Mom's head rests on Mark's shoulder, and she's crying. His arms are around her, holding her like she's precious. He murmurs something, and she looks up, tears streaming down her face. Then he kisses her softly, offering comfort.

Kisses her.

It's like a punch to the gut, and I suck in a silent breath. I stumble back, feeling...deceived, I suppose. Not only are they betraying Dad, but they're going behind my back to do it.

And it's too much with everything going on—it might be too much all on its own. I slip down the hall without them ever seeing me, sobbing silently, wishing we could just erase the last twenty-four hours and start over.

CHAPTER TWENTY-FOUR

I WAKE WITH A START. My pillow's wet with tears, but I refuse to think about Mom and Uncle Mark right now.

Prospector's Demise. The spot where Gideon Bonavit went off the cliff—that's what Caleb was so fascinated with. I told Paige's dad to check the hiking trails, but that area is away from the trails, near the cliff's edge, on a narrow wagon road that was abandoned long ago when a tunnel was blasted in the fifties, making a safer passage through the mountain.

I leap from my bed and race through the house. Thankfully, there's no sign of Mom or Mark. I can't deal with them while Caleb is missing. I just can't.

It's about seven o'clock now, and the sun is up. People mill around everywhere, all volunteers here to aid in the search. There's Division of Wildlife agents, BLM officials, and all kinds of people from the town and campgrounds.

Mr. and Mrs. Murray have a table in front of the office, and they're handing out coffee, bottled water, and snacks to the weary search teams.

Several officers I don't recognize stand with Paige's dad, and they have police dogs with them. As far as I know, our little town doesn't have any, so they must have brought them in from somewhere nearby.

Thankfully, the person I'm looking for is standing to the side of the chaos, talking with a group. I walk to Landon, and as soon as he spots me, he reaches for me.

"They're calling in a helicopter," he tells me. "They've had search and rescue out all night, but they haven't seen any sign of him."

"Prospector's Demise," I say in a rush. "That's one of the places he wanted to see. What if he didn't want to check out the spot where Gideon went over? What if he really wanted to see the canyon *below*."

Where the gold was supposedly lost.

Landon's eyes widen, and he nods, slowly at first and then with more conviction. "How do we get down there?"

———

SINCE THERE'S no real trail to Prospector's Demise, we have to make our own way through the thick brush after we leave the Jeep by the side of the closest road. It's a nasty walk, full of scratchy oak brush, prickly thistles, and sappy, low-hanging evergreen boughs.

Even though I'm wearing my hiking boots, something

sharp has lodged in the sock by my heel, just low enough I'd have to take off the boot to remove it. I ignore it as we push on.

Finally, we reach the cliff's edge.

Landon looks over the sheer wall, bracing himself. I think we're both worried Caleb might have lost his footing and tumbled off the side, but neither of us says the horrifying words out loud.

"See anything?" I ask after several long moments.

Landon shakes his head. "Nothing. How do we get down there?"

I pull out my phone, but there's no service here, therefore no way to access any of the map apps. Too bad we don't have a trail map like Caleb.

"If Caleb went this way, he probably got to this point and decided he needed to find a way down," I say, finally digging the sticker from my boot. "Which way do you think he would have gone?"

Landon looks to the left and then the right, studying the possible route along each side of the ledge. "Probably to the north—there are fewer obstacles in the way."

We follow a deer trail along the top of the canyon wall, looking for any sign of Caleb passing this way. Our path ends in a thick patch of brush that appears impossible to move through.

"I don't think he went this way." Landon puts his hands on his lower back and stretches. He only got an hour of sleep at the most, and he looks defeated.

"Let's go back to the road," I suggest. "See if we can find some sort of trail that leads into the canyon. Caleb has the map—he would have probably taken the easiest route."

I toss my pack in the back seat when we reach the Jeep. I have a few backpacking supplies with me just in case—lots of water, a first aid kit, an emergency blanket, and a handful of energy bars. It's nothing to sustain us for long, but hopefully, it will be enough to take care of Caleb when we find him.

And I say "when" because I refuse to believe this isn't the way he went. My gut tells me it is, and I pray I'm right.

He's too little to be lost. My exhausted brain dwells on all the bad things he could run into out here: bears, mountain lions, flash floods, dangerous terrain, hypothermia...

The list is too long to even contemplate.

We must find him. That's the only option.

I take off-road trails I've never gone down before, hoping one of them will take us into the canyon. Because we're forced to backtrack so many times, we're still not so far from the campground that Caleb couldn't have made it here on his bike in a few hours.

Finally, we find our road. I almost cry when we begin to descend into the canyon.

"Hold up," Landon says from the passenger's seat, looking at his phone.

"Did they find him?" I ask, relief making me nearly dizzy.

"No, but I have signal here. I need to let everyone know where we're at."

I pull over to a wide space and put the Jeep in park, practically choking on disappointment.

"Can you access a map?" I ask.

Landon sends a text, and then he waits for the GPS to load. After several long minutes, he says, "We don't have enough signal."

After another minute of waiting for it to load with no luck, Landon motions me on. We'll just have to do our best.

The road is narrow, right on the side of the cliff, just wide enough for the Jeep. I've never done an off-road trail like this, certainly not alone, and never in the driver's seat.

"You okay?" Landon looks over.

"As long as no one wants to pass," I try to joke.

We wind down, following the road, climbing over small boulders and maneuvering around tight corners.

Finally, we reach the bottom. The road runs not far from a creek. The spring runoff thankfully finished long ago. Otherwise, the trail would be a sloppy mess. Already, it's rutted from people driving through it in wet weather.

Landon cranes his neck out the window, looking at the cliff above. "Where do you think Prospector's Demise is from here?"

"When we were up there, I spotted a grove of aspens growing near the creek. Once we reach those, we'll be getting close."

But it's going to take a while at this speed. Still, even

if we're moving at a snail's pace, it's faster than traveling on foot.

"Lacey, look!" Landon says, pointing forward, nearly hanging halfway out the window.

I hit the brakes, causing the Jeep to rock back and forth, and peer ahead of us, to where Landon's pointing. He's already out the door, racing for the bike that's propped next to the road in the trees.

I slam the Jeep into park, and I'm on his heels. I don't even bother to shut the door behind me.

"Is it Caleb's?" I holler, but I already know it is.

"Caleb!" Landon shouts. He waits for a moment, and then he yells again.

Then we're silent, waiting for an answer. The only sound in the air is the gentle babbling of the creek and the sound of wind in the long grass growing on its banks.

"Caleb!" Landon yells again.

His brother's name echoes off the canyon walls.

"Maybe we should go on—"

And then we hear it. The faint sound of a whistle on the breeze—the kind hikers keep in their gear just in case they become lost. I slap a hand over my mouth, cutting myself off. The whistle stops for a second, and then it begins anew.

"That way!" Landon runs down the road, turns the corner, and then takes a sharp right into a narrow area that cuts into the canyon wall.

We both run, shouting Caleb's name.

And then there's George, running for us, tongue lolling out, happy as a giant, drooling dog can be.

"Where's Caleb, George?" Landon asks. Since we're not in an old black and white television show, George doesn't immediately turn and lead us to him. No, instead he stops to sniff a bush.

We pass him, figuring the dog will follow eventually. The whistling is louder, and then finally it stops altogether, and we hear a small voice yell, "Landon!"

And we see Caleb, with his dirt-smudged face and scratched up legs, barreling for us, running as fast as he can.

Landon races ahead and catches his brother around the middle, scooping him up and hugging him tightly.

Caleb sobs against Landon, desperately relieved.

Landon pulls him back. "What were you thinking?" he all but yells.

Without waiting for an answer, Landon pulls Caleb back into a hug. Between telling him how happy we are to find him, he scolds him for taking off. The whole time, Caleb blubbers "I'm sorry" over and over.

I stand back, not even realizing I'm crying until the tears start dripping off my chin.

When the three of us finally get control of ourselves, Landon demands, "What were you doing?"

Caleb glances at me. "I was looking for the spot Gideon Bonavit crashed."

Landon flashes me a look and then turns back to his brother. "Why would you go alone? And in the dark?"

"We're leaving!" Caleb yells, his eyes welling up with tears again. "You said you'd take me next weekend, but we're not going to be here!"

Landon points at him, still overcome with conflicting emotions. Relief wars with anger and residual fear. "That doesn't make it okay to take off on your own, and you know it!"

Caleb sags and nods his head.

"Why didn't you come back when it started getting dark?" I ask. "Wasn't it scary out here all by yourself?"

The little boy puffs up, pretending to be brave though I can tell it was the worst night of his young life. "I was going to come back, but that dumb dog wouldn't budge after it got dark." He points at George like he's the dark villain of a melodrama.

Landon closes his eyes and rubs a hand over his face. Gaining control, he looks back at Caleb. "Why didn't you leave his fool self here?"

Caleb gulps, not able to look his older brother in the eye. "I didn't want to go back by myself. Plus, the road was a lot easier to come down than go up."

The thought of riding a bike up that winding, rocky road sounds awful.

"Are you hungry?" I ask, remembering the supplies I brought with me. "Hurt? Thirsty?"

"I brought water and granola bars, but I finished them last night." He points to his tent, which he's set up so it's hidden in a nook in the rock wall. "But I was safe enough in the tent. I even brought a few blankets so I didn't get too cold."

"Come on," I say, motioning for him to follow me. "I have food and water."

"I'm going to pack up his stuff," Landon says.

I nod and take Caleb to the Jeep. After I have him set up in the back, I leave him for a few minutes so I can help Landon.

I find him sitting on a rock next to Caleb's tent, bent over, head in his hands.

"Hey," I say, kneeling next to him.

He looks up. His eyes are dry, but his expression is one of pure anguish. Maybe for the first time, he's let himself think of all the things that could have happened to his brother while he was out here alone.

"He's okay," I say quietly.

Landon nods.

I take his hands in mine and wrap my fingers through his. "Are *you* okay?"

He lets out a long, controlled breath. "Yeah, I'm just... I don't know. Exhausted, I guess."

"Do you have service? Have you called your parents?"

Landon shakes his head. "Nothing down here."

"We'll tell them as soon as we can." I get ready to stand, but Landon holds me steady. "*Lacey.*"

He only says my name, nothing else. But there's a lot in the single word.

I wrap my arms around him. He clutches me closer, needing me as much as I need him.

I've let him in, come to care too much. And not just for him, but for his family too.

Again, I've gone and fallen for a summer boy. Again, it's going to end in nothing but heartache.

I pull back after a few short moments, but only

because Caleb's waiting. Landon doesn't resist, and together, we head back to the Jeep.

Caleb's on his second bar by the time we return.

"Just so you know, little man, you're in so much trouble," Landon says as he tosses Caleb's pack and bike in the back. Then George leaps in, somehow cramming himself into the limited space.

Caleb thinks for several moments and scratches the side of his neck. "Do you think we could keep going, see if we can find Gideon's gold? You know, since Mom probably won't let me come back?"

Landon slowly turns, giving Caleb a look that makes the boy flinch.

"Or maybe not..." Caleb says.

For the first time in hours, I crack a smile.

CHAPTER TWENTY-FIVE

SLOW AND STEADY, the Jeep crawls over a particularly rough and rocky part of the road. We're just about to start climbing the canyon. I feel like I've pretty much mastered this four-wheeling thing, and I'm wondering why the boys make it sound so complicated, when my back left tire starts wobbling in my rearview mirror.

I slow to a crawl—an impressive thing to do when you're already going under five miles per hour—and watch in horror as the tire deflates and hangs loosely around the wheel.

"What was that?" Caleb asks, noticing the Jeep slowly tilting.

I growl and smack my hand against the steering wheel. Honestly, can one more thing go wrong today?

"Flat tire," I say, putting the Jeep in park and getting out to inspect the damage.

Yep. Flat.

I cross my arms and scowl at it until Landon comes to my side. The thing is, I don't actually know how to change it. Paige does—her brothers taught her when she was twelve. Uncle Mark tried to show me too, and I paid attention—I really did—but he might as well have been talking Greek.

Maybe this four-wheel thing isn't for me after all.

Landon looks like his lack of sleep is catching up to him in a big way. He's dead on his feet.

"At least you have a spare," Landon points out, already moving for it.

"Do you know how to change it?"

Landon nods and gets to work. I dig out the lug wrench, remembering that was a vital part of the whole operation.

It doesn't take Landon long to jack up the Jeep and remove what's left of the old tire.

Caleb watches with avid interest and asks me, "Why do you think it went flat?"

"I don't know," I answer, not really up to speculating at the moment.

"Was it a rock?"

"I don't know."

"Maybe there was a rusty nail in the road—like something from an old wagon!"

"*I don't know.*"

Landon tightens the lug nuts one by one, slowly releases the jack...and then he curses.

"Mom says you're not supposed to say that," Caleb so helpfully announces.

"What's wrong?" I ask, scooting Caleb back before Landon completely loses it.

Landon lies back on the hard, rocky ground. His arm is flung over his eyes. "Your spare's flat."

"How is that possible?" I demand. "It's just been on the back of the Jeep. I haven't used it even once."

"It happens. You have to check them when you check the rest of your tires."

I'm about to tell him that I don't check any of my tires, but then I realize that's probably what got us in this predicament to begin with, and I decide it's best to keep my mouth shut.

"Now what?" I ask.

He flings his arm aside so he can look at me. "Now we hike to the top of the road and see if we can still get cell signal up there.

Hike up the canyon.

It's going to take us hours. We haven't had nearly enough sleep for this.

But we don't have a choice.

We grab the rest of the water out of the Jeep, and each of us shoves a few energy bars in our pockets. George hops out of the back, and up the road we go.

Caleb, who's just as tired and crabby as we are, loses wind after the first fifteen minutes.

"Are we near the top?" he asks.

"No," Landon answers.

"When will we reach the top?"

"I don't know."

"Can I wait in the Jeep?"

"*No*," Landon and I say together.

He pouts and whines until Landon reminds him it's his fault we're out here in the first place. After that, he's pretty quiet.

George trots back and forth, staying close. Every few minutes, we look at our phones.

Pass a boulder...*no signal*.

Pass a prickly weed growing in the middle of the road...*no signal*.

Round a bend...*no signal*.

We stop for water often, and we eat another bar at midday. It wouldn't really be that bad of a hike if we'd just gotten some sleep last night. But in this condition, it might as well be Everest.

Finally, near the top, Landon lets out a happy groan. "Two bars," he says triumphantly as he raises his phone into the air.

Then he stumbles toward a boulder at the side of the trail, sits down with another groan, and dials his dad. Two seconds later, he says, "We found him."

The message is relayed, and I can hear the happy cry on the other end.

"But we're in the canyon below Prospector's Demise, and we have a flat." Landon pauses. "No, the spare is flat too."

He nods a few times, and then he hangs up.

"Well?" I ask.

"They're coming for us."

I sit on the rock beside him and let my head fall on his shoulder. Caleb lies on the ground, which is a mistake because George decides he must investigate. Caleb yelps as the dog hangs his jowly face over Caleb's eyes. Landon laughs and wraps his arm around my back, leaning on me as much as I'm leaning on him. We stay like this, exhausted, for several minutes before we begin the trek back to the Jeep.

Luckily, it's a lot easier to go down the trail than up.

Caleb has gotten his second wind, and he hurries on ahead of us, racing George to the bottom.

"We haven't really talked about me leaving," Landon says quietly, his eyes on the trail.

I glance at him. "I'm not sure what there is to say."

I don't want to talk about it—I don't even want to think about it. I want to pretend it's not happening and live in the moment.

"You have another year of school," he says.

I nod.

"And I want to take a year to continue traveling with my family. But next year, we could pick a college. Go together."

"I can't." I keep my eyes on Caleb and George.

"Why?"

"You know why. They need me here. How will they run the campground without me?" Again, I'm reminded of what I saw in the living room this morning, and for a moment, I think Mom can just go ahead and fend for herself. But that's not right either.

Landon sets his hand on my arm, pulling me to a stop. "They could hire someone to come in and help."

"No one knows this place like I do," I argue. "And

this was my parent's dream when my dad was alive—I'm not going to abandon it."

"But what's your dream, Lacey? What do you want out of life?"

I refuse to answer because I don't know. My future's always held the same thing—Gray Jay, the campground, our mountains. Even thinking of something else feels like betraying my family. Especially my dad.

Landon searches my face, growing frustrated. "You told me when we first met that you've never seen the beach—that more than anything, you want to go to the ocean."

"I *do*," I say. "You just...don't understand. You can't understand. Your family travels everywhere, sees everything, but you have no roots. You *abandoned* your roots. Obviously, they don't mean as much to you as they do to me."

We shouldn't be having this discussion right now. We're tired, we're hungry, and the last twenty-four hours have been filled with nothing but worry and stress.

But we *are* discussing it, and I don't know how to get off this train before we crash.

"So, you're never going to go anywhere or do anything? You're just going to stay here, stagnant, even though it's not what you want?"

He doesn't necessarily say it harshly, but the words still sting.

"I don't know, all right?" I say, whirling toward him. "But for now, yes, I'm here. For the foreseeable future, yes, I'm here. I don't know what you want me to say."

He studies me for several moments, and then he deflates.

"This was a mistake," I finally mutter under my breath.

I don't really mean it—but I'm tired and on-edge. And really, really mad. The problem is, I don't know who I'm mad at. I'm taking it out on Landon, but he's not the problem. I'd like to say Mom and Uncle Mark are the problem, but that's not quite right either.

Perhaps I'm mad at myself, at the fact that Landon's right. I'm never going to go anywhere or do anything. For the rest of my life, I'm going to live in the campground office, watching happy families come and then leave for their next adventure. And that thought is really, truly depressing.

But I don't know how to fix it.

"Maybe it was," he says softly, and I stiffen.

He wasn't supposed to agree.

So now what?

I can't take it back, tell him I'm sorry for the hasty, heated words—not when he feels that way.

We finally reach the Jeep and Caleb crawls in the backseat and promptly falls asleep. Landon and I sit side by side on a rock ledge near the road. Neither of us speaks as we wait for someone to come rescue us.

Eventually, the Calvary comes. Lots of Calvary.

We're surrounded by over a dozen happy, happy people. Landon's mom hugs me, thanking me for helping find her son. Caleb wakes up, and she cries grateful tears while she scolds him.

Uncle Mark stays to fix the Jeep, and I catch a ride back to the campground with Paige's brother. I glance at Landon before I slip into the passenger seat of Trenton's truck. He turns to me and jabs his hands in his pockets. He looks as miserable as I feel. Still, neither of us speaks.

After a moment, I get in the truck and close the door.

CHAPTER TWENTY-SIX

YOU'D THINK after all that, I'd sleep like the dead for the next several days. I don't.

It's three in the morning, and I'm staring at the ceiling, wondering how things went from good to awful so quickly. And, of course, I'm replaying everything in my head, making different choices.

But it makes no difference now.

There's no going back. Landon's family leaves tomorrow. I haven't seen him since the day we found Caleb in the canyon.

It's as I'm lying here, so desperately wishing I could take back what I said to Landon, that my phone chimes with a text.

Are you awake?

My chest constricts, and I stare at the words on the screen...wondering if I should even answer.

Yes.

Meet me at the gazebo in five minutes.

Five minutes doesn't give me a whole lot of time. I toss back the covers and slide my feet into the flip-flops by the side of the bed. Then I throw on a long cardigan over my shorts and sleep shirt and hurry outside.

Landon's already waiting for me. It's probably where he was when he sent the text.

My thin cotton outfit isn't suited for the cold night air, and I hug myself to keep warm.

"Don't say anything," he says, stepping forward. "Just let me talk."

I purse my lips, not sure what to expect.

He sets his warm hands on my upper arms, but he doesn't pull me any closer. "I don't regret coming here or meeting you. It wasn't a mistake. *You* weren't a mistake."

Then his hands move from my arms to my cheeks, and he presses his lips to mine. It's a middle of the night kiss—firm, desperate, far too short.

"Take care of yourself, Lacey."

And then he's gone. I watch him walk away, my mouth parted, hand reaching out to stop him, but what magic words can I say to change the circumstances?

Paige said you have to date at least three guys before you find your forever. Maybe she's right.

Or maybe Landon was my forever, and it was just our timing that was all wrong.

Either way, Landon's gone.

PAIGE POKES her head in my bedroom and frowns. "Hey."

I roll her way. "Hi."

"You're still in bed."

"I met Landon last night at three."

Her eyebrows rise, and a smirk brightens her face. "Do tell."

I roll my eyes. "He just wanted to say goodbye."

She sits next to me, frowning. "That's it?"

I nod.

"So, you guys are...over? Just like that?"

"I guess so."

My friend searches my face, looking for signs of doubt. "They're just packing up the last of their things," she says slowly, her tone more hesitant than I'm used to. "If you hurry, you could probably give him a proper goodbye. Maybe one where you don't end this so abruptly?"

I stare at her, wanting to pull the sheets over my head.

But I don't.

"Do you think I should?" I finally ask.

"I think if you're going to do it, you need to hurry."

And that's all it takes. I'm up, scurrying around my bedroom, trying to find clothes. I don't even care if they're clean as long as they're not pajamas.

"Leave it!" Paige coaxes when I pick up a brush to tackle my hair. "You don't have time. Just go."

I stare at my reflection in all its bedhead glory, and then I realize she's right. I grab an elastic band and twist my hair up as I run out the door.

I jog down the campground road, praying they're still here. People call greetings, asking why I'm in such a hurry, but I only wave. I round the last corner, out of breath and panting, and then stumble to an abrupt stop.

The Tillmans and all their bikes, tents, dogs, and kids are gone. The site sits vacant, just as clean as the day they arrived.

I choke back a sob and resist the urge to sink to the ground.

Slowly, I walk back to the house. Halfway there, I realize they might have stopped at the office before they left. On wobbling legs, I run for the parking area, silently begging them to be there.

But the parking lot is empty. I turn toward the road and just catch a glimpse of the Tillman's RV as they turn onto the highway, heading away from Gray Jay, onto bigger, better things.

CHAPTER TWENTY-SEVEN

"DAD SAYS we can have the boat again this Friday," Paige says, sitting in the chair beside me, eating a stick of licorice. "You want to come?"

The "we" in that sentence is her and Jarrett. They are honestly, officially, *finally* together. And with summer drawing to a close, Tanner's gone—and good riddance. Thomas's family left yesterday too. I'm not sure if Gia ever won him back or not.

I can't say that I really care.

"I don't think so," I tell her.

She narrows her eyes. "I know you're still all heartbroken, but you can't keep moping around all the time."

Technically, I can.

"Come on. Trenton's coming too."

"So?"

She gives me an exasperated look. "Trenton's fun. You like him."

"Are you really trying to set me up with your brother?"

Paige makes a horrified face. "Ew—*no*. I just want you to leave the campground."

"I'm going to have to pass."

She points at me as she walks toward the door. "You have one more week to walk around like a zombie, and then I'm staging an intervention."

"Goodbye, Paige," I say, rolling my eyes.

"Oh." She pops her head back in the door. "Dad wants to know if your mom would be willing to take us school shopping again this year?"

Just the thought of my mother makes me clench my teeth.

"Something up with you and your mom?" Paige asks, noticing my expression.

"No, we're fine," I lie. "I'll ask her later."

"Okay..."

I look up. "I'm fine. We're fine. Everything's fine."

She raises an eyebrow.

I sigh. "Honestly."

Without further argument, she slips out the door, informing me she'll call later. I return to the reservation sheet in front of me and answer the phone when it rings.

"Hi, hon," an elderly female voice greets me. "This is Gretchen at Site Twenty-seven. We've noticed that Twenty-nine has been empty for several weeks now, and we were hoping we could switch spots. There's a lot more afternoon shade over there."

"Twenty-nine's not available," I say rather sharply, and then I soften my tone. "Sorry."

I know it's ridiculous, but I can't bear to see someone else in it. Not yet. Soon Mom or Mark will figure out I've been keeping it vacant, and then they'll make me an appointment with a therapist. But until then, it's not going to anyone else.

———

"I'M THINKING about hiring someone to help in the office when you go back to school," Mom says as she flips through a stack of mail.

I glance at her and take another bite of cold cereal. She knows how I feel about hiring someone.

"Mark stays too busy, and I'm hoping that I'll sell more after the art show."

Things are going well for her. Mr. Albert commissioned five more pieces yesterday.

"Okay," I finally say.

She sets the mail aside and puts her hands on her hips, turning toward me. "All right. Why are you acting so irritated with me? At first, I thought this moodiness was because Landon left, but it's been weeks."

I pick up my bowl and dump the leftover milk down the sink. "I'm fine."

"You aren't fine. Tell me what's going on."

Slowly, I turn to her. I know I shouldn't, but I just can't help myself, so I say, "Is that what we do? Talk about the big, important things in our lives? Because I'm pretty sure we don't."

She catches me by the arm before I walk out the door. "Enough of this. What's going on with you?"

"Maybe a better question would be what's going on with you and Uncle Mark."

She rears back like I slapped her and opens her mouth like she's going to say something. But no words come out.

I give her several moments to come clean, brace myself for the inevitable excuses. Shaking my head, sick of just about everything, I walk out the door.

"Wait, Lacey," she hollers after me.

I almost don't turn back, but there's something off about her voice.

"You got something in the mail." She holds out an envelope, but she doesn't meet my eyes.

Hesitating, I stand here, wondering if going back now will ruin my dramatic exit. It probably will, but I don't get mail, and curiosity wins.

I take the envelope from her and frown when I see it has no return name or address. As I'm studying it, trying to decide if I'm going to open it now or later, Mom softly says, "I'm sorry."

From the corner of my eye, I see how she nervously shifts.

"You weren't supposed to find out—" she silences me with a hand in the air when I start to snarl. "*Because we knew it would hurt you.* We didn't want to tell you if it was something fleeting."

"What about Dad?" I demand, lowering my voice.

Her eyes soften, and she shakes her head. "He's gone, Lace. He's been gone for eleven years."

"But Mark's his *brother*."

She gives me a helpless shrug. "These things just happen sometimes."

Not to us. To other people—messed up people. We're supposed to be *normal*. Maybe a little broken, but normal nonetheless.

Are they going to get married? Am I going to have to live with them both under the same roof? Mark's around all the time, but it would be different.

And what if they decide to have more kids? Mom's only thirty-eight. It's not impossible. Then my sister or brother would also be my cousin.

If that's not dysfunctional, I don't know what is.

"I'm sorry we hurt you," Mom says. She sets her hand on my cheek like she used to do when I was little. "I really am."

"I know." And I mean it. I don't think she ever meant to cause me turmoil, but it was inevitable. "Now what?"

She shakes her head. "I don't know."

"Are you guys...together now?"

Slowly, gauging my reaction, she nods. "I think so."

Yuck.

"Okay," I say, tapping my palm with the envelope. I start to turn away, and then I look back, sensing this is a good time to test the waters. "What if I wanted to go away to college? Or just leave Gray Jay completely after I graduate?"

Her face falls. "Because of Mark and me?"

"No." A little bit maybe. "Because of *me*."

"You don't have to stay here, Lacey. I grew up here, loved this campground with all my heart. I knew when your grandparents wanted to sell, I had to have it. Your dad shared my vision for this place. But that doesn't mean our dream is yours. You need to do what you feel is best for *you*."

"Really?"

She crosses her arms, cracking a smile. "Well, everything might fall apart when you leave, but we'll manage."

Maybe hiring someone to help in the office will be the first step.

"And even if you leave for a while, years even, it doesn't mean you can't come back to Gray Jay down the road."

I think about actually leaving—packing the Jeep and taking off on the road I've seen so many people disappear down. Could I do it? Am I brave enough to say goodbye to the only place I've ever called home?

"But you have plenty of time to decide," she points out. "You have to graduate before I'll let you go."

Laughing, I shake my head. "I kind of figured that."

"I love you, Lacey." She pulls me into a hug. "I'm sorry if I've relied on you too much, made you feel like you could never live your own life."

My eyes mist up, and I nod. I'm about to leave, but now that we're talking—or rather, now that I'm talking to her—there's a question that's been burning inside me for weeks.

"Why did you want me to date Landon so badly? Didn't you realize it would end like this?"

Her face softens. "Can I be honest with you?"

I almost tell her it would be a nice change, but I purse my lips and nod.

"You were driving me insane with your spreadsheets and laminated charts." She smiles to soften the words. "After Thomas, you holed up in the office, working all the time. I just want you to be teenager while you still have the chance."

I cross my arms, narrowing my eyes, almost smiling. "My laminated chart is awesome."

She laughs—really laughs—and shakes her head. "I know."

We're both quiet for a few moments, pensive. Finally, sensing I'm at my emotional quota for the day, she says, "I've got to get to the studio."

I nod. She squeezes my shoulder and then walks away. I stand in the yard, all alone, feeling lost. Everything I've ever known is changing.

After a moment, I rip open the envelope. My breath catches, and I bite my lip to keep from breaking down.

It's a postcard. Landon's standing on a sunset beach, smiling. His arm is slung around a girl's shoulders, and she's looking at him, laughing. She has reddish brown hair, freckles across her nose, and eyes that are the exact shade as my mother's.

He used photo manipulation software to put me in the picture.

"Wish you were actually here," is scrawled across the

back in a masculine mix of print and cursive. "All my love, Landon."

All his love.

I blink a few times, shove the card in my pocket, and march my way to Site Twenty-seven.

"Gretchen?" I ask when I see an older woman sitting in a chair under her awning. With the way the site is situated, they're mostly in the sun.

"Yes?"

"You guys can have Twenty-nine if you still want it."

"Is it available?" she asks, her face lighting up.

I nod and shove my hand in my back pocket, feeling for the postcard. The Tillmans are far away, enjoying the coast. They're not coming back anytime soon.

And that's okay.

It has to be.

CHAPTER TWENTY-EIGHT

"YOU HAVE MAIL," Mom says the minute I walk into the office. She waves a plain white envelope in the air. "It looks just like the last one. Who are they from?"

My heart starts beating faster, and I snatch the envelope from her.

"Landon?" she guesses.

I mumble incoherent words and leave the office, heading for the house. As soon as I'm in my room, I sit on my bed and stare at the envelope.

Slowly, I tear it open and pull out another postcard. Landon's at another beach, this one rocky. Again, we're together.

He's using pictures he took of me and purposely posing himself just to make them fit together with a few tweaks.

That's insane.

That's...

So Landon.

This time, the back reads, "Still wish you were actually here. All my love, Landon."

———

"ANOTHER ONE," Mom says, motioning to the stack of mail. She's at the kitchen table, drinking coffee, waiting for me to come home from school. Big, fat snowflakes fall just outside the window, and our Christmas tree stands in the corner, all dressed in red and gold.

"This one's red," she says conversationally. "He must have been feeling festive."

I slide open the card and smile as soon as I see his name.

I finally worked up the courage to call Landon not long after he began sending the cards. We talk almost every day now, but that doesn't keep him from writing. His messages have gotten longer and longer, and now he usually sends several sheets of paper along with his postcards.

There's something very personal and sweet about hand-written letters, especially when Landon is so enamored with technology.

"So where are you now?" Mom asks.

"Louisiana," I tell her.

She takes another sip of her coffee. "I bet it's warmer there than here."

I smile. "It looks like it."

———

THE BEST THING about graduating high school is that my afternoons are now free to stalk the mailman. I wait until he's gone, and then I hurry to the box.

I've become obsessed with checking the mail. You wouldn't believe the places I've been to in Landon's cards —the California coast, the Balloon Fiesta in Albuquerque, state parks in Texas where trees drip with Spanish moss and alligators sun themselves on walking trails.

Every week like clockwork, a new card shows up. Every week, I fall a little more in love.

I have forty cards, and right there on top of a stack of bills and credit card applications sits number forty-one. I open it eagerly, hoping with all my heart the Tillmans have changed their course and are coming back this way.

Before I pull out the card, something else slips out. I read it, wondering what in the world Landon's sent me.

And then I brace myself with a hand on the mailbox. It's a plane ticket to Florida.

Landon's bought me a plane ticket.

With shaking hands, I pull out the card. Landon's once again on a beach, just like in the very first card, but this time, he's by himself.

When I flip the card over, it's blank. The usual letter is missing as well.

"I couldn't figure out a clever way to ask you to join me," an achingly familiar voice says from behind me. "So, I figured I'd just deliver this one myself."

I whirl around, clutching the plane ticket and card to my chest.

He's here.

Right here.

In Colorado.

"Landon," I breathe, overwhelmed.

He shows me a matching ticket. "I have one too, in case you're wondering. I figured we could fly together."

I throw myself at him, clutching him so tightly, I'm not sure he can breathe. "What are you doing here?"

"Are you kidding?" he says against my hair. "Gray Jay is the happening place to be in the summer. Don't you know that?"

I breathe him in, savoring his soap and laundry detergent scent.

"Will you come with me?" he asks, his voice softer and a tad bit hesitant.

"To Florida?" I ask.

He nods. "My family is there too. They miss you. Caleb's been looking for the fountain of youth."

I laugh, surprised he thinks I might turn him down. "Yes, Landon. I will go to Florida with you."

"Unless you'd rather go cave spelunking than lie on a sunny beach." He graces me with a rotten grin. "I know how much you enjoy that sort of thing."

I pull back so I can meet his eyes. "Honestly, I'd even go explore caves with you. I'm so glad you're here."

"I missed you." He brushes his knuckle against my cheek.

"I have a whole stack of postcards with photographic proof that I've been with you the whole time."

"You have been." His grin turns crooked, and he taps his chest. "Right here."

"That was the cheesiest line ever." But I laugh despite myself.

He pulls me against him. "But did it work?"

"Yeah, kinda."

Before he beats me to it, I wrap my hand around his neck, pull him closer, and kiss him.

"Have you figured out where you want to go to school?" he asks, letting himself get distracted by trivial life decisions.

"Nope." I tug him back.

"Do you think we should talk about that?"

"Eventually."

He finally gives in, and we forget about school and responsibilities.

We'll deal with all that later. Right now, all I know is Landon's here, and I'm not going to let him slip away again.

After a few moments, he jerks as if remembering something and digs his phone out of his pocket. "I almost forgot."

He holds it up, capturing the two of us in the frame.

"What are you doing?" I ask, grinning at the image of the two of us together.

"Isn't it obvious?" He kisses me again and snaps the picture. "It's for next week's postcard."

———

BONUS SCENE

Landon

"I want out," Caleb, my youngest brother, announces, twisting in his seat to look behind us at the office. "Why can't I go with Mom and Dad?"

"I don't know," Hunter says, his nose buried in his phone like usual. "Maybe because they told you to stay here?"

My thirteen-year-old brother got stuck in the middle this afternoon, between Caleb and me, so he's been especially caustic.

Caleb turns his eyes to me, begging me to give him a different answer. Though I'd like nothing more than to disagree with Hunter, I can't. I'm just opening my mouth to tell Caleb to be patient when my sister's dog coughs from the seat behind us. Something about it sounds off.

I turn around, resting my elbow on the back, and look at McKenna. "She okay?"

McKenna stares at the miniature dog with a worried expression. "I think so."

Unable to mind his own business, George sticks his head over the back of the seat. Most people would shy away from him and his drool, but McKenna doesn't mind —it's why she gets the backseat all to herself.

Candy coughs again, but this time it turns into a gag.

Hunter finally looks up from the game on his phone and turns in his seat. "What's going—*dude*. That's not right."

And for once, I have to agree with him. The dog hacked up some seriously nasty, rainbow-colored yuck. "What did she eat?"

McKenna's chin wobbles. "I gave her some of the rainbow candies."

"Rainbow candies?" I demand, shocked. "Why?"

Instead of answering me, she talks to the dog, asking her questions like the little beast will actually respond. A half-empty bag of candy sits on the seat between McKenna and her dog. Giving up, I turn around, trying to figure out how to best deal with this.

"I'm not cleaning that up," Hunter says, holding up both hands. He'd back away if he could, but he's still trapped between Caleb and me.

My youngest brother—opportunist that he is— dramatically covers his mouth. "I'm gonna be sick. You gotta let me out."

"You are not," Hunter scoffs.

Caleb then proceeds to fake gag, which makes

Hunter yell at him to knock it off. As the two argue, I step out the door.

I stick my head into the office, zeroing in on Mom and Dad. "Apparently McKenna fed Candy half a bag of rainbow candies on the drive, and she just threw up in the back seat."

"McKenna or Candy?" Mom asks.

"Candy. Now Caleb says he's going to be sick if I don't let him out." My gaze moves to the girl behind the desk. She watches me with wide eyes, horrified. And why wouldn't she be? Some entrance, Landon.

She's pretty, I think when I should be listening to Mom. *She's tall, like Evie, but she's not as curvy and her hair isn't the same color of brown.*

In fact, she doesn't look like Evie at all. She looks real, I guess. She might have makeup on—maybe some of that black mascara stuff, but I think that's it.

I bet she wouldn't leave you to make small talk for thirty minutes with her parents while she finished getting ready for a date.

The thought makes me feel guilty—unloyal even. I've been with Evie for so long, it's strange to think those thoughts about another girl. But I'm not with Evie anymore.

Mom's asking me to walk Candy and Caleb to our site. Sensing my opportunity, and seeing the empty stand on the counter, I ask the girl for a map.

Her eyes fly to the stand, and she blanches. "I just ran out. Let me print you one real quick."

"No worries," I find myself saying. "Why don't you show me the way?"

My gut tightens when she just stares at me. I thought it was clever, but maybe it hinted at desperation? It's been too long since I've had to worry about these things.

"Sure," she finally says, and then she darts up, nearly tripping over her chair. Her cheeks go pink, making her even prettier. She mumbles some trivial information to my mother—shower times and so on, and then she makes her way to me.

"I'm Landon." I hold the door open for her.

Looking straight ahead, almost as if she's avoiding looking at me, she says, "I'm Lacey."

"So, you work here?"

As soon as I say it, I want to kick myself. Of course she works here—she was sitting behind the desk. *Idiot*.

She gives me a questioning look, one that has my attention moving to her pursed lips. Because there's no recovering, I brush it off and wait for her to answer.

"My mom owns the place," she finally says.

Even better. That means she'll be here all the time.

She's checking me out, letting her eyes sweep over me, though she's trying to be nonchalant about it. I hold back a pleased grin and lead her to the Suburban.

One thing's for certain, I think as I glance again at the girl by my side. *My summer just got a lot better*.

————

ABOUT THE AUTHOR

Shari L. Tapscott writes young adult fantasy and humorous contemporary fiction. When she's not writing or reading, she enjoys gardening, making soap, and pretending she can sing. She loves white chocolate mochas, furry animals, spending time with her family, and characters who refuse to behave.

Tapscott lives in western Colorado with her husband, son, daughter, and two very spoiled Saint Bernards.